Insane Reno

Jossie Marie Solheim

Raven Crest Books

ISBN:
ISBN-13: 978-1480071209
ISBN-10: 148007120X

DEDICATION

In loving memory of John Defrates

CHAPTER 1

The car clattered across the cattle grid leading on to Davidstow airfield. Over the crashing of metal, I was sure I heard a low moan escape my mother's lips and looking at her, I noticed that her arms were pulled tightly against her sides. Her palms, which had been resting lightly in her lap, now gripped each other fiercely in a killer embrace.

I watched as my father's hand instinctively reached out, coming to rest lightly on her leg and giving it a gentle squeeze, as if to reassure her.

"This will be good for us," he said, his soft hazel eyes gazing at me in the rear view mirror, "a fresh start" he added, when neither my mother nor I responded.

"You could have a horse," he continued, "or a lamb perhaps, like your mum used to."

I looked to my mum, but she said nothing, just gazed straight ahead, as if in a trance. I looked down at her hands and saw her nails pressing deeply into her soft porcelain skin.

Then, sensing my father's eyes watching me, I turned, certain I saw a flicker of concern before he resumed his ramblings.

"That little lamb was pure white. It followed your mother everywhere, earning her the nickname, Mary.

"We all raised lambs back then of course; had to,

because there were always lambs that needed bottle feeding in the spring. For most of us, it was just a job, but your mum had never had a lamb before. She mothered it, and it naturally grew attached to her. What was it called again dear?" He asked.

"Yes! Bumble! That was it," he said, as if mum had offered him the answer.

I turned and gazed out the window, trying to process what was going on. Mum had loved our little cottage in Bude and I knew she would be upset about leaving it behind, however she seemed more than upset; it was as if she were afraid.

Although dad was trying to be positive and upbeat, as he always was, there was an unmistakable tension about him as well.

All I knew was we were moving to an area where my parents had grown up, on Bodmin moor, to a house that had been left to my mother in her family's will.

As Crowdy Reservoir passed by, I turned my attention back to mum.

My mum prided herself on her appearance, keeping her chocolate hair up in a neat bun at all times. She wore little make up, but swore by expensive skin creams, and always wore dresses that reached to her knees, or lower. She had dark brown eyes that became almost black when she was angry, but was polite and to the point at all times. In short, we were nothing alike.

Floral dresses were not for me, and if I wore skirts at all they were above the knee and as short as I could get away with, shorter, once I was out of mum's sight. The rest of the time I preferred hipsters and low cut tops. My hair was long, falling just below my waist and I loved its natural chocolate colour and waves, which softened my face. My eyes were a soft hazel, inherited from my father, and my figure was a little more rounded than my mother's, no doubt, due to my penchant for chocolate.

If I had to describe my mum in one word, it would be obsessive, because that's exactly what she was, especially when it came to being the image of the perfect housewife. She baked, grew roses, and to further the image, had a perfect little thatched cottage on the outskirts of town. Naturally, I drove her insane, refusing to be the perfect daughter she longed for, and instead rebelling at every turn.

I turned to look at my father, still chatting away to himself in the front seat. He was the glue that held our family together, the compromiser, the entertainer. He was impulsive, fun, and incredibly supportive. He doted on mum and me, showered us with gifts and surprises, and always did his best to let us know how much he cared about us. But lately, things had changed between mum and him. Now when mum was angry, his playful affection did not instantly put a smile on her face, but instead seemed only to anger her further. No longer did they spend hours talking, and sharing the ups and downs of their day; instead dad would arrive home to an empty house or just me, mum having found something more important to do.

I watched dad slowly slide into depression, despite the fact that he did his best to hide it from me, while mum silently slipped farther away from us both.

Then dad lost his job. Mum fumed, dad yelled, but the instant they heard my key in the lock they turned their backs on each other. Dad rushed to greet me, while mum did her best to ignore us.

Then, one day I came in and mum was crying, and for once she did not try to hide it. I assumed the worst, ready to believe they were splitting up. Then dad turned to me and although there was concern in his eyes, he smiled and said, "We're selling the house and moving to the moors. I'm going to start my own practice. Your mum's not very happy about it, but we have no choice. We can't afford to keep this place. Your mum inherited an old farmhouse with some land and outbuildings up on the moors. We can use the money from the sale of this property to get it fixed up and set up a clinic. I know it will be a big change for you, what with being so far from your friends and living in such an isolated area, but it makes sense," he paused and took a deep breath, "You'll still go to the same school and whenever you want to go into Bude all you have to do is ask."

So, here we are, moving to a new home. My mum is sat in the front acting like a fruit loop, and my dad is doing his best to act as if everything is fine, which clearly it isn't.

I began rummaging through my bag, searching for my iPod, in the hope of tuning them out, when suddenly dad said, "Well, this is it ladies; home sweet home."

I lifted my head and stared at the house, off in the distance. My father turned the car over the cattle grid and down the long drive, while I simply froze in my seat. This was not just any new home, it was Insane Reno.

CHAPTER 2

"Insane Reno, are you mad?" I cried. "You know what happened here, don't you?"

"It's just a house Tiz," my father said, using my nickname, "What happened here was a long time ago and the man responsible is behind bars, maybe even dead by now. It's perfectly safe."

"If he did it," I growled. I had heard all the stories about Insane Reno, knew there was speculation as to whether they had the right guy.

"He did it," my father snapped, losing his cool, which was unusual for him.

"How do you know that?"

"The stories you have heard are just rumours, that's all. The kids who started them were just trying to make the place as scary as possible. What happened here was tragic, but the man responsible was caught."

"So you expect me to believe that some guy with the mind of a child was able to commit all those murders and get away with it for so long. Please!" I hissed.

"Enough!" My father suddenly snapped. "This is it, our new home, whether you two like it or not."

As we pulled up outside the house, mum began to shake. I looked at my father but he was ignoring us both, climbing out of the car, and slamming the door behind him.

I glanced out of the car window, gazing at the old granite farmhouse with its crooked roof and cracked tiles; the garden, overgrown with weeds and surrounded by a low, stone wall. The wooden roof of a well showed above the long grass and brambles. Looking at my mum, I noticed her gaze was concentrated on the well and not the house.

"Mum, what's wrong?" I asked, genuinely concerned.

"You stay away from that well," she snapped, suddenly ripping her seatbelt off and spinning round to face me, "I mean it, you stay away from it."

"Ok," I said, holding up my hands in mock surrender.

"We're not staying," she said, turning back in her seat, but it no longer felt as if she was talking to me, "we're not," she cried, "He doesn't get it, he doesn't."

"Doesn't get what mum?" I asked, leaning closer.

"We're all gonna die Lizzy, all of us, it won't stop till we're all dead," she said, her eyes wide and bloodshot.

"Mum it's just stories," I said, repeating dad's words, needing to believe them, myself.

"It isn't, it's true. This house, it's cursed, it won't stop till we're all dead," she cried, tears gushing down her face, "All of us Lizzy, every one of us. That's what it does. I thought I got away, but it's brought me back. He's brought me back!" She snapped, stabbing a finger towards where dad stood, talking to an elderly man.

"Who, dad?" I asked.

"No!" mum snapped, grabbing her bag, as she jumped from the car and stormed off down the drive.

Dad looked up at the sound of the door slamming. Seeing mum, he hurried after her, grabbed her arm, and pulled her off to one side. I watched them through the rear window. Mum was pulling frantically at her hair, while dad tried to pry her hands free.

I shook my head, tired of their constant arguments.

Part of me wished my mother would just go away and leave us alone. I hadn't always felt that way, but lately mum seemed to turn everything into a drama, seeming always to be looking for a fight, and I'd had enough.

I looked back at the house, full of nervous tension, mingled with an unshakeable curiosity. This was the closest I had ever been to it and the thought that this would now be my home was, in some ways, an exciting one.

I could imagine what my best friend Calvin would say when I told him, the things he would ask. I would become a curiosity in school, too. Everyone would want to know what it was like to live here.

I caught movement, out of the corner of my eye, and glanced towards the front door of the house, noticing the old man my father had been talking to stepping inside. I longed to go in, but fear was holding me back. What if the house really were haunted, either by the ghosts of the murdered or the ghost of Insane Reno himself?

'Bite the bullet,' I thought to myself, 'I've got to go in there sometime, might as well be now.'

Every muscle in my body tensed as I stepped from the car, slowly moving towards the gap in the stone wall. I paused in front of it and gazed up at the old house, silently thinking 'please be nice, please be normal.'

I glanced at the edge of the wall, noticing some rusted hinges, and wondered what the gate, which had clearly once hung there, had been like.

I shivered, as a cold breeze caught my hair, and then watched, as it rushed off through the tangle of brambles, playing boisterously with an old, tattered carrier bag, which had caught in the thorns. My father's words came back to me. "The moors," he had said, whenever I asked what it was like to live here, "they're beautiful Tizzy; wild and untamed. Sometimes, it can be a glorious summer's day, the sun shining and the birds singing, and yet there can still be a strong breeze that whips through your hair, making you feel alive," I looked up at the clear blue sky, shielded my eyes against the sun, and thought how perfectly that described today.

Moving through the gate, I followed the little path of granite slabs, pausing briefly where a second, slightly thinner, path branched off to the well. I wondered why my mum was so afraid of it. To me, it just looked like any ordinary well, with its little, wooden roof and stone base. In the stories I had heard about the house the well had never been mentioned, only some of the upstairs rooms, where, supposedly, all the murders had taken place.

Shrugging off mum's words as further signs of her newly evolved, delusional self, I continued along the path, ducking beneath the ivy that hung from the roof of the open-ended porch.

I gazed at the wooden door, with its little, square window and large, plain, iron knocker. Curling my fingers around the cool handle, I took a deep breath, holding it, as I slowly eased the door open and peered inside. It was not how I had expected at all. The room before me was light and airy, with dark wood beams, hugging the ceiling, and bright, white walls.

Where were the cobwebs, the dark gloomy corners, and dingy walls that I had imagined? Instead, there were smooth, dark grey, slate tiles on the floor, two simple wooden doors that hardly screamed run for your life, and one quaint window, through which I could see tendrils of ivy, swaying in the wind.

I'll admit I was slightly disappointed. I had built up an image in my head; had prepared myself for it, and instead I had what seemed to be a perfectly normal house.

I moved towards the stairs, determined to seek out some horror; but, hearing a creak of floorboards above, I changed my mind and instead lifted the iron latch that held the door, to the left of the stairs, closed.

On opening the door, I was again met by a simple room, this one L-shaped, but painted the same simple white, and brighter than the hall, due to the four windows; one of which looked out towards the well, two over some fields at the side of the house, and the fourth looking out across the open moors to the rear, where I could see a herd of moorland ponies, grazing. The floor in this room had been newly carpeted with thick, navy blue shag and against one wall was a simple, somewhat old-fashioned, fireplace.

I headed back out into the hall, gazing up the stairs briefly; again filled with a sense that someone was watching me. I listened for a moment, but heard nothing, and shaking it off as just paranoia, I headed for the door, opposite the front entrance. Again, it was held closed by a simple iron latch that opened with ease, when I pressed on one end.

Before me was a spacious kitchen, the beams overhead, hung with long-dried herbs and plants, which, from the look of them, had been here long before the last occupants had met their untimely end; however, not everything in this room was old. The kitchen units were a light wood and modern in design. A butler sink sat under a large window, opposite the door, and looked out over the moors, where the ponies still stood grazing in the sun.

The units ran down the two longest sides of the L-shaped room; those closest to me running to the door and those across from me running down to what, I assumed, was an eighteenth century version of a bay window with large, granite pillars, between the frames.

Inside of this bay, a window seat had been built and scattered with soft cushions. Next to this, flicking out into the foot of the L, was a large window that looked out over the farm yard and its outbuildings.

A large wooden table sat at this end of the room that looked like it had been in the same spot for years. The table was set with two thick, wooden benches, running down the longer edges, and a single chair at each shorter end. It had been positioned in front of a giant inglenook fireplace.

I was awestruck by the space, with its mixture of modern and old. The fireplace with its small nooks and crannies for pots and pans impressed me the most. I moved across to it, stretching up a hand to the large, stone mantle, then leaning in and opening the cast iron door set into the chimney breast on the right hand side. I'd seen bread ovens like this in books, but had never actually seen a real one, before.

I lifted my hand up and trailed it over the large, copper pans that hung from hooks, above the old Rayburn, which sat right in the middle of the recess, and wondered if all these things were remnants of the previous occupants' lives.

I was impressed with my father's handiwork; amazed by the little details he had added, to perfect the traditional look, right down to the wicker basket that sat to the left of the Rayburn, full of chunky logs, and opposite that, a cast iron bucket, filled with matching tools. It suited my mother perfectly and I could picture her baking away in here; a clean, crisp apron, tied around her waist.

I turned my attention to the small passage beside the large inglenook, noting that it sloped upward, ending in a couple of small steps and a tiny door. Just in front of the passage, and to the side, there was a large set of double doors, leading out through a tunnel of white honeysuckle, to the yard.

I realised, as I stood there gazing around me at the large, homely kitchen, that my father had been right, this was just a house, a beautiful one at that, and there really wasn't anything for me to be afraid of here.

Before I headed for the passage, I moved back across the kitchen, wanting to reassure myself that we had all the mod cons. I was relieved to see a modern cooker, opposite the sink, which I had missed on first entering the room.

I pulled open the cupboards, wondering if, somewhere, there was a hidden fridge or freezer, but found nothing and decided to see what was hidden behind a door that sat dead centre at the top of the L. Inside I found a small room with no windows and assumed it to be a utility. The walls, once again, had been painted white; the floor, the same slate slabs that ran from hall to kitchen. There was nothing to excite me here, so I closed the door and made my way back to the small passage.

I moved along the passage, placing a hand on the smooth, cool wall and watched, as it slowly climbed higher with each step. There were no windows, here; so it had more of a gloomy feel than the rest of the house, but I was not afraid.

Reaching the steps, I lifted the latch on the small door, revealing a tiny room with only one small, round window, at head level, in the back wall. Ducking under the doorframe, I moved across to the window and gazed out over the front yard; noticing that my parents were no longer stood in the long driveway, squabbling.

The ceiling was low in here and I could touch the thick, wooden beams, overhead with ease. Turning, I noted that the main feature of the room was a large, open fireplace, which sat beside the door, emitting a welcoming glow that enveloped the room with its warmth and which, combined with the dimness of the room, gave it a cosy feel.

I looked up, as I heard the latch of the door being lifted, and smiled, as dad stepped into the room; ducking, so as not to bash his head.

"Oh, you found the den, already," he said happily, "I'd hoped you hadn't, but never mind."

"It's nice," I replied, "but, why is the floor raised up in here?" I watched my father's eyes flicker towards the fireplace then down to the floor. I thought I saw a glimpse of unease, but it was gone in a flash and he simply shrugged.

"Guess they just wanted to make it cosier," he said.

*

We were standing in the kitchen, mum pressed tight against the sink, staring at the passage that led to the den.

"Everything has been fixed," my dad said, pacing back and forth, in front of the double doors that led out into the yard.

He looked towards me and continued, "I know what happened was difficult for you, but I need you to trust me. Nothing is going to happen, I promise you," he was choosing his words carefully, ever conscious that I was listening.

I racked my brains, trying to remember everything I had heard about this house. I knew there had been seven people killed here; their murders spread out over several years.

Eventually, a man with Down's syndrome was arrested. It was rumoured that he'd been tricked into giving the farm to a friendly couple who had promised to take care of him for the rest of his life; but, who had, in fact, treated him like a slave. To get revenge, he had killed them, only to find that they had not left the house to him as they had promised, but instead had left it to some distant relatives.

Angered further, the man killed again and once again was duped out of his home. In a final rage, he murdered two adults and a boy, before being found, covered in blood and clinging to the second child, a girl, in an upstairs bedroom.

Some said he was preparing to rape her, others that the young girl had been so kind to him that he simply could not bring himself to kill her.

I had never heard a name mentioned for the girl or any

of the victims, but the man was always referred to as Insane Reno; the house, I assumed, eventually inheriting the name.

I turned to look back to my mother, now sobbing in my father's arms, and could not help but wonder if she had been that little girl. I watched as my father stroked her hair, trying to soothe her.

"Just try for us," I heard my father whisper in her ear, "it's safe, I promise you," I watched as he lifted her face up, forcing her gaze from the passage, "Please," he pleaded.

"I can't," she replied simply, "I'm going home, I've already called Donald to come and collect me. He's on his way as we speak. I'll wait for him at the end of the lane," she said, matter-of-factly, and then, giving me a nervous glance, she headed for the hall.

I stood silently urging my father to go after her, but he simply turned his back to me, his shoulders shaking, as he broke into tears.

CHAPTER 3

I sat in the bay window of my room looking out across the moors, the tops of Rough Tor and Brown Willy, visible in the distance. The last three days had passed by in a hurry. Dad and I had been working tirelessly to arrange the empty house and make it a home.

We did not talk about mum, despite the fact that I was bursting with questions, nor did we talk about the house or its history.

As the bare rooms were slowly filled with our furniture, the fears I'd had about the house began to vanish. There was nothing scary or evil about this place, anymore; either upstairs or down. Although once, a horribly deranged man had wreaked havoc here, he was now safely locked away in a mental institution, where he would remain for the rest of his life; if it had not already come to an end, of course.

I got up from the window seat and glanced around my room. It was long and thin with two large windows along the right hand wall that looked out over the farm yard and, of course, the large bay window, looking out over the moors. The walls were white and there were dark wood beams crisscrossing the room, high above my head.

My furniture, brought from the cottage, was all white and consisted of a single bed, a desk, one bedside cabinet, a large wardrobe, two shelving units, and a small television stand, on top of which sat my flat screen.

I had worked hard each evening, when finished with the rest of the house, on making my room my own and now had a collection of old teddy's that I had cherished since childhood, books, and a few other bits and pieces scattered around. I liked it and I was happy.

Hearing a car, I slid off the seat and moved across to my bed, clambering over it and sliding the window open; shivering a little, as the brisk moorland wind sailed in. Leaning out, I turned my head, trying to see what was coming.

I spotted an old, red truck, bouncing its way down the drive, the owner clearly oblivious to the mass of potholes.

I caught sight of my father, coming out of the smaller of our two barns. This was the one that had been deemed the most suitable for his new practice. He was wearing blue overalls, covered in paint, and raised a hand in greeting to the new arrival.

I assumed this was our new farm labourer; although, as of yet, dad hadn't bought any livestock. Unable to stand the cold breeze any longer, I turned, sliding the window closed. Deciding dad would be distracted for some time, I moved across to my laptop, switched it on, and pulled out my desk chair, determined to do some serious research on the happenings at Insane Reno, all those years ago.

Bringing up the search engine, I typed Insane Reno into the small bar and clicked enter. There were plenty of hits and, as I scanned through, I realised that most of them were people discussing the tale in different forums.

I scanned some of these half-heartedly, but it was just the same old stories I had heard time and time again.

One sparked my interest a little, but only because it mentioned the fact that lots of action had been going on at the house. It was posted just a month ago, so the action mentioned was clearly nothing more exciting than workmen, coming to prepare it for our arrival.

Dad had arranged for the whole interior of the house to be fixed up, before we moved in, taking a small loan in order to pay for it, a loan he'd intended to pay back when our old house was sold; although, how that would work, now, with mum living there, I was not altogether sure.

Going back to the main search, I skipped through page after page of useless gossip. No one seemed to know the name of the surviving victim.

I racked my brain, trying to remember anything my parents might have said that could give a hint as to what had happened here, but there had been nothing; no mention of mum being in a house while her family was massacred. But, bearing in mind the fact that my mum hadn't even let me watch the news till my sixteenth birthday for fear I would find it too distressing, mass murder in the family was not a topic she was likely to discuss with me.

It was clear that her family must have been the ones killed; but, whether she had lived with them on the moors or with someone else, I had no idea.

I had always assumed that she had lived with her parents. I knew that they had died in a car crash when mum was young and that mum had gone to live with my father's family, at some point. There was a chance that this was after her parents died; but what if it wasn't? What if she had gone to live with these relatives then seen or heard them be killed?

The only problem was with the boy in the stories. They said that he was the girl's brother; but mum didn't have a brother, at least not one that she had ever talked to me about.

What I needed were newspaper reports on the murder. If mum was connected then it had to have happened in her lifetime. She was forty-one now; but it was safe to say that she would have been a child, when it took place.

I was about to go back to the search, when there was a

firm knock on my bedroom door.

"Who is it?" I called, hurriedly snapping my laptop shut.

"Who do you think it is?" my father asked, pushing the door open, "There's someone I'd like you to meet," he added hurriedly, then stepped into the room, holding the door wide.

A tall, muscular man with short, dark hair strolled into the room; his hands in his pockets and a comfortable smile on his face. He nodded in my direction, his dark brown eyes, locking onto mine.

If I believed in love at first sight, I might have mistaken my feelings for it; but I was sensible enough to know that it was lust, not love, that had just kicked me in the stomach.

"This is Jem, our new farm hand," my father said.

"Hi, nice to meet ya," Jem replied, in a deep, sexy voice that made my heart skip a beat.

"Hi," I managed to reply, somewhat dreamily, and instantly felt like an idiot. I saw Jem smile, as if knowing the effect he was having on me, and instantly tried to recompose myself.

"My daughter, Tiz," My dad said, using my nickname. I could have killed him.

"Tiz?" Jem said, rolling the name around on his tongue, as if trying to get a feel for it, "Why, Tiz?"

"My name's Lizzy," I hissed, glaring at dad, "Tiz is just a nickname I got because..."

"Because she likes throwing tizzies," my dad interjected. I could have died.

"Oh, she's fiery then?"

"More so than the pits of hell," my father continued, "so watch yourself; wouldn't want you getting burned now," he added, then dodged out of the way of my shoe, which I had yanked off my foot and aimed at his head.

"See what I mean?" he added, and scurried out of the

room, calling over his shoulder, "And if that had hit me madam, you'd be grounded for a week."

"You wouldn't last a day," I called after him.

"We'll see," he called back and then thundered down the stairs, chuckling to himself, as he went.

"He's an idiot. Ignore him," I said, getting up and moving past Jem to the door. "Not being funny, but I've got work to do," I added, resting against it and gazing up into his big, brown eyes, noticing his long lashes, and then slowly flicking my gaze down his body. He was well built, but it was clearly all muscle, and he was around six foot, at a guess.

"Well, I wouldn't want to keep you," he said, stepping out the door; then, turning his head and smiling, he added, "but, just so you know, you ever lob a shoe at me, I'm gonna have ta get you back," my mind raced with all the ways he could possibly mean and every part of me wanted to ask, 'such as?' But instead I simply smirked and slammed the door in his, far too sexy, face.

No! I was not going to be giggly or girly or, even for a second, let him think that, just because he was hot, he could have me just like that. It just wasn't going to happen. Still, I got the feeling he might be fun to have around.

CHAPTER 4

I was sat in the kitchen sketching, when Jem next crossed my path. He strolled in through the back door, as if he owned the place, spotted me sitting on the window seat, my legs curled beneath me, and headed in my direction. I hurriedly snatched my pad away, clutching it to my chest, and frowned, as I watched a smirk spread across his face.

"That bad, eh?" he asked, grinning, as he dropped down beside me.

I rolled my eyes and stood up, brushing a strand of hair from my face, as I debated whether to stay and be sociable or seek solitude in my room.

"Don't smell anything cooking, what times tea?" He continued, scratching lazily at his stomach.

"You'd have to ask dad," I replied.

"Your dad's the cook?" He gasped, eyes wide.

"Yes. Men do cook you know," I replied, talking to him slowly, in an attempt to hint at the idiocy of his response, but he seemed not to notice; simply staring back at me with a bemused smile. "There are lots of famous male chefs," I continued, "In fact, nowadays, you see more male chefs on television than you do women."

"This isn't television and your dad isn't some puffed up, bossy idiot, who stands around all day yelling orders. He's an everyday bloke, working hard to support a family;

a family that seems to consist of one doodling girl, who can't be bothered to get off her butt and show her father she appreciates all the hard work he does. Hard work, I might add, that enables you to have everything your pretty little heart desires," he said, then added, "but don't worry, go back to your doodling and be sure to give a shout if you need anything," he jumped to his feet at this, bending at the waist in a bow, and added, "after all we wouldn't want madam to break a nail."

Doodling! How frigging dare he suggest I doodled? Ok, his statement had bigger issues than this, but they would be harder to argue, after all he did sort of have a point.

"Doodle! Frigging doodle," I snapped, getting right up in his face, "I am top of my class in art, I do not frigging doodle," I growled, flipping open the pad to the first page and thrusting it into his face. "That is not a doodle," I hissed.

He took a step back, glanced at the pad, and replied, "No, you're right, it's not *just* a doodle," I frowned, fighting the urge to smash him round the head with the pad, as he emphasised the just.

"What do you mean by just?" I hissed.

"What I said," he replied smugly, then reached out a hand, snatching up a cushion from the window seat and, holding it towards me, asked, "What's this?"

"It's a cushion," I replied, rolling my eyes.

"But it ain't, is it? It's not just a cushion. It's a blue and white, stripy cushion and that," he continued, pointing to my sketch, "is not just a doodle, it's a doodle of a naked man," he added, laughing raucously.

"It's a sketch of a naked man," I corrected, refusing to play his stupid game and trying to remain calm, "A doodle is something someone does absentmindedly, when chatting on the phone. That took more than a couple of minutes, hours in fact. It's not a doodle."

"Fine," Jem said, holding up his hands in mock

submission, "It's a sketch of a naked man. It's good too, although you could have been a bit more generous in the tackle department," he added.

"It's to life. I can't help it if he was lacking in that area," I replied, and watched him burst into fits of laughter.

"So, do you do everything to scale?" He asked, snatching for my sketchbook and flipping through it, to my horror.

"Don't!" I said, diving for it, but he simply stuck out his hand to stop me and, as hard as I fought, I could not get past him to my pad.

"Well, there must be something real embarrassing in here; either that or you've been sketching me," he said. I froze, instantly realising my mistake.

"Oh my god, you have, haven't you?" He said, standing on tiptoes, as he began to thumb through the pages.

I jumped for my pad, once more, but it was no good, he was too tall.

"Please," I begged, but it was too late. I could tell by his eyes that he had found it.

"Wow! This is amazing," he said, seriously.

"Do I really look that good?" He added, with a wry smile.

'Better,' I said to myself. To him, simply, "I told you, I draw what I see and that's how you look," I was just grateful that he was a man with an ego; too busy revelling in his own vanity to notice the fact that I had paid particular care to his muscles and his sexy eyes.

"You did this when I was chopping the wood," he said, stating the obvious. "I gotta be careful what I do within sight of your window," he joked, "I mean, this is near photo quality."

"Well, I told you I was top of my class," I snapped.

"So, is this what you want to do?"

"No, this is for fun. I want to be a vet, like my dad."

"Wow! Ambitious," he said, teasingly, "mind you, the fiery ones always are."

"I'm not fiery," I snapped, and then at his wry smile, I snatched my pad from his hand and stormed out of the room.

"Hey! What about my grub?" I heard him call after me.

"Cook it yourself!" I yelled back.

CHAPTER 5

I made my way downstairs, pausing in the hallway; certain I had seen something move past the small glass window in the front door. Shaking it off as paranoia, I turned and made my way into the kitchen, where Jem stood, chest bare, with a tea towel slung over his shoulder.

"You should draw me like this," he said, not even looking up, "That way, every time you try to call me a pig, I can remind you just how good I look, playing chef."

I scowled at his back, sliding into a chair at the table, "The last thing I need is a reminder of you dripping sweat in my tea," I replied, getting back up and moving across to get a look at what he was cooking.

"Oh, highly impressive, a stir fry. My god, how skilled you are."

"Hey, at least I'm attempting to cook something, not like little miss thing," he added, snatching the tea towel off his shoulder and flicking it at my retreating behind, "Don't smile," he called, "your face might crack."

I scowled at him again, heading for the cupboard, where the dishes were kept; determined to do something, so he did not think I was a complete waste of space. His harsh words earlier had struck a chord with me. I'd never thought about how little my parents made me do; had never needed to before, as my mother had always taken care of the house, while my father worked to support us all and, although I would never admit it to Jem, he had a point. I did need to do more to help around here. The only problem was I didn't have a domestic bone in my body.

I could sense Jem's eyes on me, as I laid the table, so I added a little extra swing to my hips and bent over a little further than was necessary, as I set each dish in place.

"Your thong's showing," my dad said, making me jump out of my skin, as he strolled into the kitchen, sniffing the air.

"Something smells good," he added, dropping into his seat, at the far end of the table, and gazing at me with a wry smile.

"Did I interrupt something?" He asked.

"I dunno, did he?" Jem said, directing his question at me, as he beamed like a Cheshire cat.

"No!" I snapped, mortified.

"Guess not then," he replied, "must have just been my imagination, playing tricks on me," he added.

"What are you on about?" I growled.

"Oh nothing, it's just I could have sworn you were doing your best model swagger, and making an extra point of flashing me you're..," he paused, mid-sentence, and looked to my father.

"Thong," my father replied, with a laugh.

"Well, I was gonna say cute little butt, but thong works," he added and joined in with my father's laughter.

"Oh, very funny," I snarled. "Anyway, what gave you the right to look?"

"If you wiggle it at me, I'm gonna look."

"I didn't frigging wiggle it," I hissed.

"No, but you wanted to, and that counts," he replied, the smug smile, still firmly in place.

"Dad!" I cried, "Are you gonna let him get away with that?" I said, knowing instantly what his reply would be.

"Hey, you were flashing him your thong, so you can

fight your own battles."

"So, if I flashed my thong at a stranger and he grabbed my butt, you'd be ok with that?" I asked.

"I dunno," he replied, then leaning back to look at Jem he added, "Hey Jem, why don't you try it and see."

"Dad!" I cried, quickly dropping onto one of the bench seats, as Jem turned, eyes full of mischief.

"Don't worry, I'll get ya later," he said, rubbing his hands together, then turned back to the cooker, switching the hob off, and scuttling towards the table, frying pan in hand.

Dad licked his lips excitedly, as Jem tipped a huge portion of his beef stir-fry onto each of our plates and then lobbed the frying pan into the sink from where he stood.

"Ya could have broken that," I snapped, but Jem just smirked and dropped down onto the bench beside me, giving me a playful nudge with his elbow.

"This is great," dad said, already chomping on his first forkful.

"It's alright," I said, not wanting to bolster Jem's ego, too much.

"Stir-fry's are easy, any old muppet could make one, but if you want real food, you should try my mum's roast dinner; my god its heaven, in fact, pretty much everything she cooks is," Jem said.

"Oh, her pasties are the best," my father interjected, "Proper, gravy filled, pasties that just melt in the mouth, nothing like 'em."

"She sells them now, alongside her eggs and chickens. Pockets the money for herself, 'cause dad doesn't give her nothing."

"Your dad always was a bit tight on the money. I remember when we used to go to the pub together, he refused to go in on rounds, just bought his own drinks and that was that," my father replied.

"Nothing's changed," Jem said with a smile, "happy enough to accept them from us, but won't ever return the favour."

"Sounds about right," my father said, "How's your sister?"

"What, Morwena? She's good. She's studying for her exams, at the moment, driving mum insane 'cause she doesn't want to study."

Dad looked to me at this and smiled. I rolled my eyes, knowing what was coming next, the proud father routine.

"Well, Tiz is doing great with her revision. Maybe she could help encourage your sister," my jaw dropped.

"Yeah, maybe," Jem replied, looking at me with a smirk.

"Just bring her over sometime," my dad continued, "It'll be fun, won't it Tiz, and nice for you to meet someone your own age around here."

I let out a sigh and simply nodded; then glared at Jem, who was staring across at me, a wide grin on his face.

"Well, I'm gonna head out to the barn for the night," Jem said, getting to his feet and after a few hurried goodnights, he was gone.

"Why won't he sleep in the house?" I asked my father.

"Superstition," he replied, "His family have helped on this farm for years and they have all refused to live in the house. They say the house has a bad omen. Still, the little rooms above the barn are quite nice and he has more space out there than he would in our spare room," he said, standing and picking up his plate.

I followed his lead and stood there, while he washed the dishes, taking each one from him, and drying it slowly.

"There are a lot of people scared of this house dad," I said.

"Jem's not scared of it," he replied, "For him, I think it's more about having his own space."

"Mum was though," he turned and looked at me then,

a sad smile on his face, "Your mum has her reasons, but they're based on fantasy not reality," he said.

"Fantasy?"

"Well, sort of. They're not founded. They're based on her own fears. You know the stories about Reno. Well, your mum, she sort of believes them, I guess; but it's like I said, the man who did those things, he's been caught. Nothing is going to happen to you here, I promise."

I watched him closely. How could he expect me to believe that? Yes, mum was a drama queen; but she had been genuinely afraid of this house, scared enough that she had left.

"What are you thinking?" My father asked, gazing into my eyes.

"That mum wouldn't have left us like that; not if she wasn't genuinely afraid."

"Your mum has other reasons for leaving us Tiz, and it isn't that she doesn't love you, she does, it's..," he paused, turned back to the sink and shrugged his shoulders, "it's just me she doesn't want anymore," he added.

"It's Mr Thomas, isn't it?" I asked. "Dad, he's an idiot, she won't stay with him."

I'd seen how mum was with Mr Thomas, had even suspected that there might be more to it, and hoped that now dad would confirm it.

"I don't want to talk about this Tiz," he said firmly, stuffing the last plate into the rack, "Your mum isn't going to come back. She has her reasons and, as much as I wish I could change her mind, I can't. She is and always will be there for you."

"I hate her!" I snapped, and I meant it. For months, the hate had been building, but now it was like a fire inside of me, eating away at me.

"No you don't Tizzy, she's your mum, she loves you and you love her. You're just disappointed in her right now and that's ok."

"How can you be so nice to her, after what she has done to you? Dad, she's been having an affair!"

"No she hasn't, your mum isn't like that. She's living back at the house, not with him. Yes, she is close to him, but she won't do anything with him, not till we are officially over at any rate."

"And are you over, dad?" I asked.

"We've been over for a long time Tiz. We just weren't ready to admit it before," he replied.

"Tell me what happened here dad, to the last family I mean," I added.

"Come on, let's go through to the den, it'll be warmer in there," he said and led the way.

The den was one of my favourite rooms in the house, especially now that we had furnished it. We had kept it simple, placing two large, soft, tan coloured chairs in front of the fire with a small table in between, on which was a simple lamp. The chair closest to the door had become dad's chair, the other, mine, and we each had a bookcase beside us. Behind us were three oak filing cabinets. It was our cosy little bolt hole, a place to hide away at the end of the day and it was perfect.

Dad sat in his chair and I dropped into mine. I crossed my legs beneath me and gazed over at my father expectantly.

"You've heard the stories about this house and for the most part, they are true," he said, "but, like all stories, fiction gets mixed up with fact," he added.

I nodded, not wanting to interrupt.

"This house was owned by a lady called Patience. She lived here with her husband Bert and a man with Down's syndrome that everyone called Reno.

Now, the house was gifted to Patience and her husband, when Reno was 6 years old, on the condition that they ensure that Reno had a home here and was cared for, for the rest of his life. It was gifted to them by Reno's father, who was very sick and could no longer give his son the care and attention he needed. Reno's father remained at the house until his death a year later; however, when Reno was just seventeen, Patience and her husband were murdered.

The house then passed to Bert's brother, Martin, and his wife Audrey, who had a sixteen year old son, Matthew, and of course they took over the care of Reno; however, when Reno was twenty-five, they too were murdered. Matthew was away at college at the time.

Matthew naturally took over the farm, after their death, and the care of Reno. He was also the one to keep Reno out of jail, fighting tooth and nail to prove Reno's innocence. He clearly really believed in Reno; wrongly so, because, when he was forty-one and married to your mother's aunt Julie, Reno killed him and his whole family, bar one."

"Mum?" I said, and my father looked deep into my eyes, uncertainty in his own.

"I think that's enough for one night," he said, getting to his feet, "I love you Tiz," he added, kissing me on the forehead, and then hurried from the room, before I could object.

CHAPTER 6

Someone rapping loudly on my bedroom door awakened me early the next morning. I lifted my head sleepily and gazed around the room, in a daze.

"What?" I groaned, assuming it was dad; then jumped out of my skin, as the door slowly opened and Jem's head appeared.

"Hey!" I snapped, "What the hell do you think you're doing? I could have been sprawled on the bed naked."

"You're not though," he replied, with a cocky smile, "Anyway, get up, get dressed, and meet me in the kitchen in five. I'm taking you on a surprise trip, by order of your father."

I glanced over at the clock and frowned "At six am?" I snarled.

"At six am," Jem replied, with a wink, and disappeared out the door.

I jumped out of bed and rushed for the bathroom, which was next to my room, then showered and dressed hurriedly, before rushing downstairs, where I could smell something tasty cooking. Jem turned and smiled, as I entered the kitchen, then began to dish a large helping of scrambled eggs onto a plate.

"Wow! Someone likes surprises," he added, with a smile.

I scowled at him and dropped into the chair closest to the fire, so that I could watch him, as he worked.

"Your dad says, you can't cook," he said, as he sat down across from me, sliding my plate to me, "Why's that?" He asked, as he tucked into his own breakfast.

"My mum is anti-invasion," I replied, "and the kitchen was her domain. If I so much as stuck my nose in the door, when she was cooking, she'd give me hell."

"Well, you better learn. You can't expect your father to work all day, then come in and cook for us, and my contract says meals included, not meals included if you cook them."

I poked out my tongue and then tucked into my breakfast. My father had said nothing about cooking and I was in no hurry to learn. Although, a small part of me longed to impress Jem, I highly suspected that cooking was not the way to do it; not unless he had a penchant for beans on toast, microwave meals, or a simple sandwich.

I watched, as Jem stuffed the last of his breakfast into his mouth and snatched up his plate, which he then laid in the sink.

"You better get a move on," he said, glancing over at me, still only half-way through my meal. "I'll be out by the truck," he added.

I nodded, and watched him leave, then began to eat my food, double speed.

When I got out to the truck, Jem was leaning lazily against the bonnet, gazing off across the moors; seemingly deep in thought.

"You took your time," he said, suddenly. "Nice day for a drive though," he added, moving around to the driver's side of the cab and climbing in.

"Where are we going?" I asked, getting in beside him.

"You'll see," he replied.

*

Ten minutes later, we turned off the lane onto a dirt drive, surrounded on both sides by thick hedges.

Jem was whistling happily, as we bumped our way along, eventually coming to a large yard, belonging to a small, tattered, grey farmhouse, in front of which, Jem parked. Switching off the engine, he turned to me and smiled, then said, "Welcome to the madhouse."

I gazed at the old building in front of me with its lopsided porch and patchy plasterwork and looked at Jem, who simply shrugged. The whole place seemed neglected and unloved. Even Reno, with its tattered roof, peeling paint, and slightly grubby facade looked like a palace compared to this place with its broken windows, missing roof tiles, and broken guttering.

"Jem!" A large woman cried, wobbling her way out of the house in a tatty floral dress, covered with a large, off-white apron, "Just in time for some hot tea," she called, yanking open Jem's door and pulling him into her arms with one hand, while the other forced his head down into her large, jiggling bosom, and nearly suffocating him in the process.

"Two days!" She hissed angrily, flinging him away from her and giving him a clip around the ear, a smile still plastered on her round, chubby face.

"Yeah, yeah," Jem said, pulling free of her and stepping out of her reach, his hand shooting out in my direction.

"Oh my!" His mother said, her hands flying to her mouth, "Ain't you a pretty little mite," she added, scurrying around the truck, as fast as her stumpy legs would carry her, and practically dragging me from the truck; Jem's laughter ringing out behind her, as my head too, was thrust between her large breasts.

"Just like your mother," she sang, "but at least you have a little more meat on your bones," she added, grabbing at my side and clamping hold of my love handles. I was horrified and glanced at Jem, praying he had not seen; but no such luck, he was bent over double, laughing raucously.

"You must come in and have some breakfast. You're too late to catch the men. They're already off to market, bar Grandpa Derek; however, Morwena's around and driving me insane, I might add. Now, I know you girls need a break, especially with your exams coming up. I swear, all these school holidays, they're getting beyond a joke," she said, as she dragged me towards the farmhouse, "Seems you're barely back at school a day, before there's another one nearly due. Course it's just an excuse for the teachers to get extra days off, isn't it? It's those with younger children that I worry about. The teachers don't think about those that have to work; costs a fortune for a minder for you kids these days too, but you have to, don't you, if you work. Now, I've always been alright, 'cause I'm lucky enough to work from home, but poor Gracie, she has a hell of a time.

Have you met Gracie Briggs? Lovely girl, she is, but a brood the likes of which I ain't ever seen in such a young girl and they all have different fathers, 'cept the twins of course, but well, they can't, can they? I told her, she wants to put her foot down with these men, 'cause none of them shows an interest; don't even pay her no money for 'em, and they bloody should. I told her, she wants a real man, but she'll have fun finding one with eight nippers in tow," I gazed at Jem's mum, feeling somewhat overwhelmed. She did not pause once, nor did she seem to feel the need to wait for a response.

"Well, I said to Jem he should go round there and show an interest, just to make her feel better like, 'cause god forbid, and mind I'm not judgemental, but well, I wouldn't want him taking on all them kids; still, letting her think he might can't hurt. He's a strapping lad. Ain't no girl that would say no to that, eh?" She said, spinning me to look at Jem, who was now leaning against the open door of the house with a large grin on his face, "Course, Tristan is more your age; you must meet him."

My ears pricked up at this. Was this a brother Jem had failed to mention?

"Now, Tristan is nineteen and takes after his father; very silent and brooding."

"A frigging miserable git, you mean," Jem piped in.

"Now, Jem," his mother said, waving a chubby finger at him, "That's no way to talk about your brother. Granted, he ain't as bold as you, nor anywhere near as charismatic, but he has many a good point."

"If you class sneaky, manipulative, and completely screwed up as good points," Jem hissed.

"Don't mind him," she said, pulling me close, once more, then whispering in my ear, "Brotherly rivalry; it's a stinker, but it happens," she added.

I watched Jem shake his head and then turn back out into the yard, leaving me to the mercy of his mother.

"Sit, sit, sit," she said, pulling out a chair and practically throwing me into it. I glanced around at the small, cramped kitchen with its lopsided units and bowed worktops. Everything in the room looked as if it had been built from a mishmash of scavenged refuse; each cabinet and door painted a different colour, and some, garishly so.

An old butler sink, similar to ours, sat dead centre of the units, which ran down the right hand side of the room, and opposite this was a battered old Rayburn; while, in the centre, sat a long, thin table with an array of different chairs clustered around it.

At the foot of the room was a battered, old chair with grey duct tape slapped on in dribs and drabs, clearly holding the stuffing in. Beside this, sat an equally tatty dog bed in which an old collie laid, his nose buried between his paws, snoring loudly.

Jem's mum caught me gazing at the dog. "I hope he wakes up before you go," she said, "He'll go berserk trying to work out what the new smell is, if he misses you. Deaf as a post, that one," she added, and then, raising her voice, she yelled, "Soot, Soot," but the dog did not stir. "See?" She added, and returned to filling the kettle, which she promptly dropped on top of the Rayburn.

"You best not be getting on at me dog," a male voice said. I looked up to see the old man my father had been talking to, on the day of our arrival at Reno, shuffle slowly into the room; a hand pressed to his back, as if he were in pain and a dirty, old, tweed cap, slanted at an angle, on top of his head. His hair was receding from his forehead and stuck out from under the cap in scruffy, grey waves. His face was saggy and wrinkled, causing jowls to form, either side of his chin; giving him the appearance of an old, tired bulldog, the effect of which was added to by his slightly squinted, slate grey, eyes.

"Bah!" Jem's mum hissed, waving a hand dismissively, "Can't get on at what can't hear you."

"He hears," the man said, "He's just smart, 'tends he can't, so ya leaves him the hell alone," he said, reaching in his coat and pulling out something large that was wrapped in a thick wad of newspaper, "Soot, ya want this?" He said, and instantly the dog's eyes shot open.

I watched, as he removed a large, juicy bone from the paper and handed it to the dog, who took it gently from the old man's hands; his tail wagging happily, as he turned and wandered out into the yard.

"See, ain't nought wrong with his hearing."

"It's his nose there ain't nought wrong with," she replied, and turned to me, "Two old coots in this house, what with him and that dog," she said, and frowned.

"How's it going at that old house of yours?" The old man asked.

"Good, thank you," I replied, with a smile.

"Aye, 'tis a good house, despite what people think," he replied, scratching lazily at his stomach.

"That's Grandpa Derek, by the way," Jem's mum

suddenly jumped in, "and I'm Jenny. Our manners lack sometimes," she added, "but, we get there in the end."

Derek let out a long groan at this and slouched down in his seat, gazing out through the door next to his chair.

"Kipper's got something," he chirped, and patted his knees. A few seconds later, a wiry Jack Russell skidded into the room, dropping down into a sit in front of the old man; his whole bottom wiggling, clearly proud of the large pheasant, which was gripped between his teeth.

"Good boy," the old man said, reaching down, taking the bird from him, and throwing it across the room to Mrs Trerise, who caught it with ease and beamed happily.

"Now, that's a nice bird," she said, and forgetting the tea, she hurried out into the yard, the bird swinging by its feet from her hand.

She returned a few minutes later; the bird replaced with a small bone, which she chucked to the Jack, who caught it and charged outside.

"How many dogs do you have?" I asked, curious.

"Nine," Mrs Trerise replied, sliding a mug of tea across the table to me; three Jack's, four Border Collies, and two Springer Spaniels and that's not counting the pups," my eyes lit up at this. I loved puppies and had always longed to have one of my own, but mum had been so house-proud that animals were forbidden in our home.

"We've got some Jack's and some Collie pups at the moment; nice litters, too, but you'll be seeing 'em soon enough," she said with a smile, then moved across to the doorway and started to yell, "Morwena you best be out of your pit," she waited a few minutes, then yelled again, "Morwena!"

"Ma, it's half term," I heard a voice call back.

"I don't give a fig if it's half term or not. There's eggs need collecting, puppies that need feeding, and a pheasant that needs plucking. God help me; I'll string you up if you ain't down here in five minutes."

The old man chuckled lightly at this and set about rolling up a paper that was resting on the table beside him.

"Aye Mor, you best mark her words, she's armed," he said jokingly, and handed Mrs Trerise the paper.

"Aye, and I bet I know who armed her," the voice called back, sounding closer now.

A few minutes later, Morwena walked into the room and dropped onto her grandfather's lap, throwing her head back on his shoulder and gazing into his eyes sleepily.

"I'm so tired Gramps. Can't you do my chores for me?"

"Don't you dare give into her!" Mrs Trerise snapped, as the old man's eyes softened.

"I'll tell ya what," he said, stroking Morwena's hair affectionately, "I'll give ya a hand and we can get it done in half the time. How's that do ya?" He asked.

Morwena smiled, then wrapped her arms around her grandfather's neck and hugged him tight. "Love you Gramps," she said, ignoring her mother's exasperated sigh.

I looked at Morwena, noting that she was around my height with incredibly long, golden brown hair that fell down to her bum; it's thick waves, pushed back off her face, on one side, with a silver clip.

She looked across at me. Her huge brown eyes locked onto mine, as a large, warm smile spread over her face, instantly putting me at ease.

"You must be Lizzy," she said. "I'm Morwena."

I nodded and smiled; feeling nervous, surrounded by all these new faces.

Morwena slid off her grandfather's lap. She had a curvy figure, but it suited her, and she was dressed in a long, pink nightdress that had a picture of a pony on the front, and read 'I love Shetlands.' She came and sat down at the table, gazing across at me, seemingly deep in thought.

"I'm not awake yet," she said suddenly, turning and glaring at her mum.

I simply nodded.

"Does your dad make you get up like this?" She asked, watching her mum closely.

I shook my head and watched her arch her brows at her mother, "Just mine then," she said sulkily, but her mother ignored her and strolled out of the room.

Jem appeared at the door then, to my great relief, and leaned against the frame, eyeing the room with a smile.

"Hey Gramps," he said, scratching lazily at his ear, "Did you give Soot a bone?" he asked.

His grandfather nodded and waited for Jem to go on.

"Yeah, well he's burying it in mum's vegetable patch," Jem replied, laughing.

His grandfather jumped to his feet, eyes full of fear, and hurried for the door; pausing briefly beside Jem, he said, "Keep ya mother busy."

At that very moment, a loud shout rocked the house and there was a cascade of thuds, as Mrs Trerise charged into the room, snatching up a broom, and raced towards the door, where the two men were stood.

"Too late," Jem said with a grin, as his grandfather shot past him, yelling for his dog at the top of his voice.

"You best get that old mutt out of my veggies, before I string the pair of you up by ya ears," Mrs Trerise called, standing just outside the door, waving the broom above her head.

"You don't have to be mad to live here," Morwena said calmly, "but it helps."

*

Half an hour later, I stood in the yard, watching Jem lead a dapple grey mare into the back of a horse trailer that he had hitched to his truck.

"Mor," he called, "can ya show Tiz the pups?"

"Sure," she replied, then added, "Come on, they're in

the barn."

I followed her excitedly, as she led me down a small gravel path that ran between the house and a large vegetable patch to a small wooden building that, like the rest of this farm, seemed close to falling down.

Morwena gripped hold of the large, rusty metal handle that ran down the side of the door and pulled back on it with all her might, nearly falling over, as it suddenly gave way and flew backwards to reveal a small space to the right hand side of which sat three stables.

Brushing her now rust stained hands on her jeans, she stepped over a low board that had been used to block the lower half of the door and slowly began to fling open wooden shutters, flooding the small stable block with light.

"Gotta get some air in here; it's always so stuffy in the mornings," she said, as I stepped into the barn, my excitement building, as I heard the happy yaps coming from the first stable.

"Here, hand me that board," she said, pointing to a long, white piece of wood that was leaning against the wall.

"Gotta put this in or they'll be running all over the farm," Morwena said, tugging at the crotch of her jeans, before sliding back a bolt and booting the bottom of a second door that seemed determined to remain in its current position.

"I think I've put on weight," she added, matter of factly, pausing in her task, once more, to tug at the crotch of her jeans, "They're driving me mad," she added, aiming another vicious kick at the base of the door; but still, it didn't budge.

"Damn it!" she snapped, pulling her foot back, once more, and slamming it hard into the wood, causing it to crack slightly; still, it did not come unstuck.

Morwena, however, refused to be beaten, ramming her shoulder into the door and pushing with all her might.

"Here, come give this a kick, right at the bottom

there," she said, as I moved forward, then added, "On three," she moved back away from the door and slowly began to count.

"…Three," she said, throwing her shoulder into the door, while I smashed my foot hard into the bottom corner; horrified, as the door flew open and Morwena landed hard on the ground, nearly knocking the wind out of herself.

I rushed to her, eager to help, but she was already getting to her feet, laughing hysterically.

"Frigging door!" She said, with a smile, then kicked it back against the wall; snatching at a small metal hook that hung loosely from the back of it, as she secured it in place.

"Ok," she said, letting out a large sigh of relief, "Let's get this board in and the pups out," she added, snatching up the board and showing me how to slot it into place.

Then she headed across to the first stable, pulling back the bolt with a clunk and swinging the door wide, instantly releasing a pack of boisterous puppies that hurtled around the small stable block and jumped up at our legs excitedly.

"Oh my god, they're beautiful," I gasped, crouching down and reaching out to a little fat one that was wobbling its way towards me on short, chubby, little legs.

"Aye, they're alright," she said, scooping up a little, tri puppy and rubbing its nose, "I like the Collies," she added, "but the Jacks have more character."

She placed the puppy on the floor and picked up another board. Moving across to the second stable, she slid the bolt back and pulled the door open, just enough for her to slide the board into place.

"Had dad make these slots, 'cause the collies worked out how to knock the boards over," she said, pulling the door wide and showing me the slots, which matched the ones I had already seen, "Collies are clever like that. We got slots all round now; makes life a hell of a lot easier and means I can have this all open, so they get lots of light and air."

My attention, however, was quickly diverted; my gaze becoming fixed on the tiny little pups that lay inside, their ears and eyes, still tightly closed.

"Where's their mum?" I asked.

Morwena laughed and stepped carefully into the stable, prodding the straw gently. Suddenly, a few feet from her, the straw began to rustle and a little, tan nose appeared, "She buries herself under the straw when she wants a break," Morwena said, with a laugh, "She's a good mum, but she likes her own space, too," she added.

I smiled, as the rest of the little dog appeared.

"She's what they call a teacup Jack Russell."

"Yeah, I know," I said, looking down at the Collie pups that had gathered around my feet, "I saw your other Jack, too; Kipper. He's a Parson's Jack Russell, isn't he?"

She nodded and scooped up one of the Jack Russell pups gently, bringing it across to where I was stood, smiling.

"Now, the Collies are ready to go, 'least they will be in a day or two, but these, they won't be ready for weeks. Course it depends what you want, really," I looked at her perplexed, not sure what she was on about, "They're both real active breeds and both need a lot of mental stimulation. They have a lot of the same merits really, but the Jacks, they're more mischievous: crafty, more likely to think for themselves. That's not to say they ain't loyal though, 'cause they are, majorly so. Now, the Collies, they're more obedient, if you bring 'em up right, and some think they're smarter, but I disagree. Sure, they'll do what you tell 'em and learn fast, but the Jacks can learn just as fast and do just as well. They're just more independent. Both make good pets," she continued, "but, if you want a hunter, then it's gotta be a Jack. However, if it's a herder you're after, then probably a Collie; although, to be fair, a Jack can pretty much do whatever they put their minds to."

"My sister is Jack Russell mad," Jem said, walking into the barn, "Personally, I think they're equally good breeds and you're better off picking based on what tickles your own personal fancy."

"Picking?" I said.

"Yeah, picking. That's part of your surprise. Your dad wants you to have a puppy. I've already given the money to mum," he said.

"Ya did what?" Morwena snapped, "Oh great! I put in all the work and mum gets all the profit," she hissed.

"Mum pays for all the food," Jem replied, brightly.

I gazed down at the puppies, running around me, and then at the one in Morwena's hands and knew instantly that I had to have one of the Collie pups. They were just big balls of fluff, especially the little tri one, in my arms.

"Awww, she already knows which one she wants," Morwena said, and made her way back over to the pile of puppies, placing the little Jack Russell down.

When she came back, she reached out for the Collie in my arms, "I think this one's a boy," she said, turning him over, to his disgust; his little legs waving frantically in the air, as she looked him over.

"Yep," she said, smiling, "Jem, can you ask mum for a blue ribbon with Lizzy's name on it?" She said.

Jem looked at me and I beamed, "I think your right, sis," he said, before disappearing from the barn.

"You can pick him up in a day or two, all going well. Just gotta make sure they're eating and drinking proper by themselves; although, to be fair," she said, holding my new pup in her hands and raising him up and down slightly, as if guessing his weight, "I'd say he's eating more than well enough, but I'd just like to be sure and it'll give you chance to get set up, anyway," she added.

I said nothing, just simply beamed. I was over the moon. Never, in my wildest dreams, had I imagined that I would ever be allowed to have a dog, while still living at home; but then, of course, mum wasn't at home anymore, at least not our new home. I felt a slight twinge of sorrow, but then remembered how she had been lately and shrugged it off. It was probably for the best really.

Jem returned a few minutes later, a small blue ribbon in his hands, which he handed to Morwena.

"Here, hold him still," Morwena said, handing me the pup, and I watched happily, as she placed the little blue ribbon around his neck and tied it carefully in place.

"Now, it might come off," she said, "but, even if it does, we're not gonna lose him. He's the little fatty in the litter," she added, with a smile.

I hugged him to me tightly, then read what was written on the ribbon, 'Tiz'. I looked up at Jem, who simply smiled.

CHAPTER 7

"What's with the horse?" I asked Jem, as we pulled out of the yard.

"I'd have thought that was obvious," he replied, a bemused smile on his face.

"Please tell me that's not for me," I said, dreading his answer.

When I'd asked my dad for a horse, I'd been thinking of a beautiful stallion, not a tired old nag, and Misty, the rather rotund, dapple, grey I'd just watched Jem load into the trailer, definitely fell into the latter category.

"Did you pick her?" I asked, finding it hard to believe that this was my father's doing.

"Yep," he replied smugly, "she's a good horse and I'm not gonna risk sticking you on something more frisky, when I have no idea of your skill level."

"I've been riding, since I was six years old; I am perfectly competent," I hissed.

"And you're sure about that, are you?" he asked.

I nodded silently, wanting to slap him in the face.

"Where did you learn to ride?" He questioned, his eyebrows raised and a smug smile firmly fixed on his face.

I folded my arms and smiled, as I gave him the name of the stables. Although, not the best locally, it had a good reputation, was clean, and tidy, and the horses were all well cared for. It was also the stable of choice for most of the young girls in Bude.

"So, in other words," he said, calmly, "you've learnt to ride on an old hack, which needed no guidance, whatsoever, and knew all the routes by heart. Did they even bother to teach you to hold the reins correctly?"

"Now, you're just being ridiculous," I snapped, "I know how to hold the reins, how to dismount and mount, without the aid of a mounting block, and if you give me a shovel, I recon I could muck out a stable twice as fast as you, and all."

"I'm sure you can," he replied, stopping at a junction and fishing a fag out of his shirt pocket, "but stables like that one are aimed at the Emits. The only thing they're interested in buying is mild-mannered nags that can happily plod along the same routes every day with gormless emits and their bratty kids, safely sat on top. They'd certainly never dream of having a horse with even an ounce of spirit and rarely take the time to teach anyone anything beyond the basics."

"Do you have to call them that?" I asked, trying to change the subject, "I personally don't think it's very nice to call holidaymakers Emits. It doesn't even make sense, anyway," I added, begrudgingly; knowing he had a point about the stables. I had, in fact, complained about the same thing, on several occasions.

The problem was that the majority of the stables locally were designed to attract holidaymakers; most of which had little skill, when it came to riding a horse. It was also the holidaymakers that brought in the money that was needed to keep the stables running. This money meant that, often, the local girls, who could not afford to pay for riding lessons, were able to obtain them, for free, in exchange for helping keep the stables clean and for taking care of the day to day needs of the horses. Still, I liked to think I had a pretty good equestrian knowledge, despite that fact.

"Do you know what an Emit is?"

"It's a type of fly," I replied, rolling my eyes.

"Not just any fly," he hissed, "an emit is a fly that just loves horse shit and that little fly will happily fly around horse shit, all day long, without a care in the world for nothing; not the other bugs that live there, not the place where that shit rests, not even for the shit itself really. It just wants to come to a nice place and destroy it for everyone else."

"Wow, you really like shit, don't you?" I teased.

"And worse, they can't just come and visit the shit; they have to buy second frigging homes in the shit. And do you think they give a frig about the bugs that were born in the shit, that can't afford to buy property there no more, 'cause all the frigging emits are buying up everything and making the frigging prices sky rocket?"

"I had no idea shit was such a thriving place," I replied, unable to repress my laughter.

"Cornwall is to holidaymakers what shit is to emits. They're attracted to it, but they have no consideration for those that were born and raised here; hence why holidaymakers are known as emits," he snapped angrily.

"So, if they are Emits and Cornwall is the shit, what does that make those of us that were born here, tapeworms?" I asked, struggling hard to get the words out between fits of laughter. He merely glared at me and continued on his rant.

"It's the same thing every summer, they swarm down here in the thousands, stand around blocking the paths like idiots, don't let no one out when there's a mile long line of traffic, and are damn rude. Plus, they leave behind all their rubbish and act as if they own the place," he snapped, casting his now spent fag out the window and instantly pulling another from his pocket, "Scum, they are!" He snapped, jamming it between his teeth and steering with his elbows, while he sparked up.

"But, technically the fly version of an emit doesn't do all that, does it?" I said, then bit my lip, as he spun to look at me; his eyes, ablaze with anger.

I held up my hands in mock surrender and turned to gaze out the window, as I fought to control my giggles.

It was then that I spotted a herd of shaggy, highland cattle out of the truck window and watched as they slowly moved through the prickly gorse with its bright yellow flowers. These beautiful animals were incredibly large, yet with their long, thick, wavy, coats of ginger, they seemed somehow docile and pleasant, despite the two impressive horns that erupted from their skulls. I watched closely, hoping to see my favourite among the herd, distinguishable, by his own somewhat mismatched horns, one of which pointed to the sky, while the other flopped forward and indicated the ground; however, they were too far away for me to make him out.

I turned in my seat and gazed at Jem, mischief in my eyes, and asked, "So, what's your brother like?" My mouth, creasing into a grin, as he physically tensed at my words.

"My brother is in a whole league of his own. I don't like him, he doesn't like me, and we do our best to stay out of each other's way, and if you have any sense, whatsoever, you'll steer clear of him, too," he replied.

"Oh come on, he can't be that bad," I teased, "So, what, he borrows your CD's and clothes," I said, then smiling added, "or did he borrow one of your girlfriends?"

Jem laughed, "Just wait until you see him," he said, with a grin, "Not everyone in this family got lucky with their looks like Mor and I," he added, his face suddenly turning serious again, "My brother's weird. He has no emotions and doesn't care about anyone or anything, but himself. I know some people are like that, but those people at least care about their families, but Tristan doesn't. There isn't an ounce of doubt in my mind that he would sell us all out, just to get what he wants. I don't trust him and I don't like him. The only reason I even tolerate him is because he is family and that's what you do, isn't it?" He said, almost pleadingly, then paused, as if waiting for me to say no, and end his torture, "Even then, it's more for my mum than anything else; but, bar family stuff, I stay as far away from him as possible."

"Is that why you're working for my dad; I mean you're the oldest boy, right? Therefore, I'm assuming you're going to inherit your parents' farm, one day; so, shouldn't you be there working, instead of at ours," I replied.

"Partly, but it's more about having my own space. I'm never gonna be able to say that I worked hard for everything I've got, because, the truth is, I won't have. No matter how I look at it, it's all going to get handed to me on a plate, eventually," he said, taking one hand from the steering wheel briefly and rubbing at his brow, "It's good to have that security, you know, but I want a bit of independence too, something that I can do off my own back. I can't get that at home. I mean, there are four of us, all jostling to run that place, and ultimately, what my father and grandfather say goes.

Your dad is offering me more than that, a chance to be in charge of something for myself," he said, gazing at me and smiling, "It sounds silly, I know; but your dad, he wants the animals and the working farm, but he doesn't have the time to run it all, not with the surgery, and so, he's pretty much giving me free reign. It's a good feeling and having my own space feels pretty good, too," he added, beaming now, "Hell Tiz, you saw it back there, and that's only with three of them, it's crazy! Don't get me wrong, I love my family, but hell, sometimes a guy just needs a bit of peace and quiet."

I smiled as I watched him, his whole face alive with joy, and I wondered what it was like to have what you really wanted in life.

I knew what I wanted to be; had since I was a little girl.

I'd lived for the weekends, when my father would take me down to the veterinary clinic and lead me through to where all the sick animals were housed, introducing me to the ones I didn't know and smiling, when I rushed to see one of the regulars. My father was just so patient with me and very gentle with all of the animals that I had always longed to grow up and be just like him.

Back then, it had all seemed so simple. Now, with my exams well underway, it had all become much more complicated. What if I wasn't good enough? I'd never considered any other career; had always been so sure that I would follow in my father's footsteps. What would I do if I didn't make the grade?

"Penny for them," Jem said suddenly, making me start.

"Is that why you're in the barn?" I asked, thinking on my feet. There was no way I was admitting my fears to him.

"Yeah, pretty much," he replied.

"So, it's not the house then?" I asked.

"Why would it be?"

"Well, I dunno, with all the stories about Reno and you skulking in the barn, I just assumed you were scared or something," I replied, rolling my eyes, as he burst out laughing.

"Scared of a house?" He said, once he had calmed himself, "It's bricks and mortar Tiz; big, frigging, granite bricks, admittedly, but still bricks and mortar. So, people were murdered there. So what, it happens and sure; a lot of people, but it was Reno, the man that did it, not the house, plus they caught him. So, what's the worry?" He added, "Anyway, even if Reno is still alive, somewhere, he's gonna be locked up, and let's say they did let him out; well, it ain't me that's got to worry, is it? I mean, I'm just the farm hand and the dude never went after them, did he, just the..."

"Just the family inside," I finished for him.

"Tiz, the dude is either real old or dead by now, he ain't

gonna be coming back. I mean, what happened to your mum was tragic and I feel for her, but your dad's right. The house is safe; not to mention the best farm, this side of the moors. There's loads of farmers 'round here that would kill for that place, so enjoy it."

"So, my mum was there?" I said, without thinking.

Jem's gaze flicked to mine briefly; concern clearly visible, despite his best efforts to hide it, and with a sigh he pulled the truck over onto the verge. He looked into my eyes searchingly for a few seconds, then rubbed at his ear roughly.

"I dunno much about all that stuff, but I know your mum lost her family, and that can't have been easy. My gramps says that she freaked out, big time, when you moved into Reno and she ain't there now, so I figure she really dislikes that house. What I'm saying is, your mum, she has her reasons for being scared of it, don't she, and what happened, losing her family like that, it can't have been easy for her; but that house, Tiz, it ain't dangerous, it's just a house. Don't let your mum's fears scare you."

"I'm not scared," I snapped. "I just thought maybe you were; that's all," I replied.

"I just like my own space, Tiz. In the barn, I get that, and it suits me. Look, let's just get you home; get the horse settled in, and then you can make plans for your new pup. I'll even take you to the local pet shop, if you play your cards right," he said, with a smile.

*

Later that night, I sat in my room with the lights off, gazing out over the yard. It had been a long day and I was tired, but what Jem had said kept nagging at me.

He'd clammed up, I was sure of that; had taken the time to pull over and cover himself, but why not just tell me? Why turn around and say, it couldn't have been easy for her to lose her family like that?

Like everyone else in my life, Jem was treating me like a child, keeping things from me, and judging me as what, too immature to cope with reality?

I was about ready to slip beneath my duvet and close my eyes, when I heard voices coming from the barn. I watched, intrigued, as my father emerged, closely followed by Jem. I couldn't make out what they were saying; but, when Jem's arm shot out towards my bedroom window, I hurriedly ducked out of sight.

Plucking up courage, I raised my head and peered out of the window, once more. They were both still there and Jem was waving his arms animatedly. Desperate to hear more, I gently eased the handle open, pushing the window outwards, just a tad, in order to hear them.

My father's voice instantly carried to me on the wind, "I'll talk to her," he said.

"All I'm saying," Jem replied, "is that, if you don't tell her, someone else will, and surely it's better coming from you than one of the local gossips."

"I know," my father responded, "but it's not Tiz I'm worried about, it's her mother; she'd never forgive me."

"Will Tiz if you don't tell her? Look, I know I don't have kids, but I was one once, ya know, and well, if I knew people were keeping things from me, I went out of my way to work out what. Way I figure it, if you don't tell her, she'll go looking for answers from someone else. Hell, I almost told her today, 'cause I didn't have a clue she was in the dark about it all. She's a smart kid. She'll find out whether you tell her or not. I just think it's better that it comes from you."

After Jem had disappeared into the barn, I watched my father pace up and down the yard. Almost an hour passed before the footsteps receded and all fell silent.

So, Jem had been holding back on me. That girl had been my mum, which meant the boy must have been her brother, but why never mention him? If she didn't want me to know the story of his murder, then why not just tell me that he had died, alongside her parents? It just didn't make sense.

I just hoped that now, because of Jem, my father would tell me the truth.

CHAPTER 8

I woke early the next morning to find my father sitting on my window seat, gazing out across the moors. He looked at me, as I sat up, a warm smile, spreading over his face.

"Morning beautiful," he said.

"Hi dad," I replied, returning the smile.

"I had an interesting conversation with Jem last night," he said calmly, "and I wanted to talk to you, before he gets back from his family's farm," he continued.

"Me and your mum; well, we've tried our best to protect you over the years and sometimes, I guess, we misjudged things and perhaps held back on telling you stuff, because we didn't want to scare or worry you. But, I know you're smart and I know you have a lot of questions about this place and what happened here; so I am going to try to be as honest with you as I can right now, ok?"

I nodded eagerly, not wanting to interrupt him and risk him changing his mind.

"You asked me if your mum was the girl who survived the last murders and well, the answer to that is yes," he said.

I was jumping for joy inside, but did my best not to show it. My mother's fear had been too intense for it to be due to simply losing family here.

My father took a deep breath and continued," Your mum lost her parents when she was just six years old. They had gone out for a romantic meal together and on their way home another car, the driver of which was highly intoxicated, hit them. They were both killed instantly. The man responsible died later in hospital. Their names were Thomas and Mary Richards. As well as your mum, they had a four-year-old son, named Tom.

Your mother and Tom had no family in Kent and so they had to come back to Cornwall to live with your mother's aunt Julie and her husband, Matthew Yelland, in this very house. This room, in fact, was your mother's room," he added, with a weak smile.

"Your mother was very happy here and loved the moors very much, back then. She spent a lot of time with Reno and was very kind to him; which, I guess, made it very hard for her to understand why he would kill her family like that.

After the murders, your mum refused to talk about it with anyone; so it wasn't just you, Tiz. The police questioned her over and over, but she refused to say a word. My parents did their best to get her to open up; but, still she refused. However, I am getting ahead of myself.

Now, where was I? Yes, your mum. She moved in with her aunt Julie and Matthew, as did her brother, Tom.

The Yelland's were very well liked and Matthew was a very hard working man. He loved the moors and children and, although he had none of his own, he could often be found showing children around the farm. He could tell you the name of every animal, every plant, and even every bug. He was a happy, jolly man and he treated Reno like his son; even, as I think I mentioned before, defending Reno and keeping him out of jail, after the murder of Matthew's own parents.

Sadly, his faith in Reno was bad judgement and it resulted in the death of three more people, but Matthew could not be faulted; he was an amazing man and so kind. Their lives were taken when your mother was eleven. It was an incredibly hard time for her. So many questions were asked of her, but she just couldn't bring herself to talk about what had happened that night.

With no family left, your mum became an orphan. Thankfully, the community here, on the moors, is a very close-knit one and Jem's grandfather offered to take in your mother; as did my parents, of course."

"So, that's how mum ended up living with your family," I said, and my father nodded.

"People say in the stories that mum was found, being hugged by Reno. Is that true?" I asked.

"Yes, it's true. The police found them in this very room, Reno was covered in blood, clinging to your mum. They claimed that he was saying he was sorry, over and over, and that the police couldn't get any sense out of him. Your mother, as I've already said, refused to say anything at all. They said that it was the shock, but she never spoke about it, not to me nor to anyone else.

But, trauma can do that sometimes and I believe that your mum just shut it out, altogether," he said, and then sat there gazing at me.

I had so many questions; but, they were all questions I was sure my father could not answer for me.

If my mother had refused to talk about it to anyone; had, in some way, blocked it all out, then clearly she and Reno were the only two that knew what actually happened that night. There was a chance that Reno was still alive; but, even if he were, I would have little chance of actually being able to talk to him and, even if I could, I was not sure I fancied the idea of talking to a mass murderer.

On the other hand, trying to get my mum to talk would be like trying to elicit conversation from a brick wall. I thought back to the day we moved in, trying to think about everything mum had said and done, and I remembered her reaction to the well.

"Why was mum so afraid of the well?" I asked.

My father faltered for a moment, concern and uncertainty clearly etched on his face.

"I don't know," he said, at last, but I was certain he was lying.

"How about the passage?"

He shrugged, "I'm not sure Tizzy. That's something you would have to ask her," he said.

"What about Jem's grandfather?" I continued.

"Now, that I can tell you," he said, "Jem's grandfather was a very persistent man. He was determined to get your mum to open up and felt that it was in her best interest to do so; so he talked to her a lot, or tried to, but your mum avoided him, as much as she could. Of course, he was probably right. It wasn't good for your mum to keep all this stuff locked up inside, but your mum would not talk, no matter how much he tried.

Now, when I decided to move back here, it was with him that I spoke. He had been taking care of the farm, on my behalf, making sure that kids didn't break in and that it was kept locked up tight and he had done a good job of it; so, naturally, I asked him to supervise the renovations with the help of his son and grandsons.

Your mum, though, thought that it was him who had talked me into coming back here. I assume she feels that he's still trying to get her to open up about what happened here that night, although I can't be sure. Your mum avoids this house and anyone that tries to get her to talk about it.

Sadly, I made the mistake of trying to do that over the last few years and now I, too, have been pushed out of her life.

So, as much as you want answers Tiz, on this one, you are better off just letting it go. Your mum, she doesn't cope well with being reminded of this place or what happened here and there is nothing wrong with that. It was really hard for her. She was so young and she lost everything that night, so let her hide from it, if she wants."

I nodded simply, but I was not sure I could do what he asked. Like Jem's grandfather, I felt mum needed to talk. How else could she move on from it all?

I climbed out of bed and hurried across to my father, throwing my arms around his neck and hugging him close.

"Thank you," I whispered in his ear.

"For what?" He asked.

"For being honest with me," I replied, giving him a squeeze and a kiss on the cheek.

CHAPTER 9

After my father had left my room, I picked up my journal and began to jot down everything he had told me.

I paused, when I got to the part about mum and Reno being found in this very room, and gazed about me. I realised that her aunt and uncle must have been very fond of her to let her have this room. It was not only the biggest in the house, but, due to the bay windows, it was also the best, although; to be fair, with how long and thin it was, it probably wasn't suitable for a double bed.

I wondered where they would have sat and how the room might have looked back then; shivering at the thought of the bloodstains that, until recently, may have been evident in some of the upstairs rooms. I got to my feet and wandered downstairs, searching in the kitchen drawers for a tape measure. Jem strolled in, as I was searching and gazed at me with a bemused smile.

"Tape measure," I said simply, not bothering to look at him, "have you seen it? I want to know if my room's big enough for a double bed," I added.

"Wow, I know I'm irresistible, but ya don't need to go out of your way like that. I'm quite happy to share your single, as long as you don't hog all the covers."

I rolled my eyes at him and sighed, "You, Jem Trerise, are the last man on earth I would ever dream of sharing a bed with."

"Then you won't be disappointed when I tell ya that a double bed won't fit in there; but, seeing as the room was designed especially for a man's beloved daughter, it wouldn't, would it," he said and laughed.

"How do you know that?"

"Because this house was built in the 18th century by a relative of mine; an incredibly eccentric relative by all accounts, who was slightly obsessed with gambling, drinking, and smuggling, but a relative, nonetheless."

"So, you know all about it then?" I asked intrigued.

"Well, not everything, but I've heard some of the stories about the place and I do know that he built your room for his daughter; however, you'll like this," he said arching his brows, "the daughter died three years before the house was even thought of, not sure from what, but he adored his daughter so much, he built her the perfect room, despite the fact that she was dead, and turned it into a kind of shrine to her. No one, not even his wife was allowed in the room. Bit bonkers, if you ask me, but I guess Tristan had to get it from somewhere."

"Is this a joke?" I asked, finding it hard to believe anything Jem said.

"No joke. I'm deadly serious. My granddad has all the plans; diaries and all kinds of stuff that was written by the guy. We're not allowed anywhere near them, but apparently the shrine was about the only nice thing the guy ever did. He was hung in the end, at Bodmin jail, but that was after he lost this place."

"How did he lose it?"

"Got drunk and used it as a bet, forget what the bet was for, now, but whatever it was, it weren't worth loosing this place for; still, I'm guessing he realised that, when he sobered up."

I nodded, still not sure if he was telling me the truth or having me on, so I decided I would take it with a grain of salt, until I heard it from a more reliable source.

"So, why'd you really wanna know if a double bed would fit in your room?" He asked.

"I was just wondering why my mum's aunt would give her the best room in the house, that's all."

"Well, Matthew had it when he was a kid, I think, and that psychopath Reno was always down in the living room. He had a little bed and stuff, where you're dad has his office now. I figure they wanted to be able to keep an eye on him, what with his disabilities."

"How do you know so much?" I asked, "I mean, surely this was all before your time."

"Everyone knows about this house, Tiz. When you live out here on the moors you have to get used to everyone knowing your business. After all, there isn't all that much to do around here and so gossiping has become the favourite way to pass some time, and when it comes to juicy gossip, Reno sure hits the spot.

What you have to remember, too, is that there are still a lot of people living on the moors that were around back when the last murders took place and, as most of the local kids used to come up here to spend time with Matthew and his wife, it was a pretty big shock to the community, when they were killed. Mum says Matthew's wife used to cook lots of cakes for them all and that Matthew used to take the kids off over the moors, in big groups, teaching them about the plants and animals that live here. I used to think it sounded pretty boring, but she says he had a way of making everything fun.

So, you see, everyone loved the Yellands. The adults loved them, because they kept the local kids out of their hair and out of trouble, and the kids loved them, because they kept them full of tasty treats and also entertained."

"They sound as if they were really nice," I said, wondering if, perhaps, it had been jealousy that had driven Reno to kill. "Do you know what the house was called, originally?" I asked.

"Tor View Farm, I think. Not very original, is it, but I guess it does what it says on the tin," he said, with a laugh.

"Better than Insane Reno," I replied.

"I dunno; I think it has a certain ring to it," he added with a smile.

"So, do you know much about Reno, the man?" I asked.

"Not really, only that he was obsessed with Reno, the place, and that's how he got his nickname."

"Reno? Where is that?" I asked.

"America, I think. What's with all the questions, anyway?" He asked, eyeing me suspiciously.

"Dunno; just interested, really. Wouldn't you be? I mean everything that happened here and then my mum being witness to part of it, as well. I guess I just need to make sense of it and maybe, in doing so, I'll be able to understand my mum a little better, too," I said, then remembering it was down to him that my father had, at last, opened up to me, I added, "Thanks, by the way; I heard you talked to my dad. I appreciate it."

"No worries," he replied, scuffing his boot across the slate tiles, "If it's information about this place you want, you should talk to my gramps. He knows it all, and what's more, he loves talking about it."

"I might do that," I replied.

"Well, I've got work to do," Jem said, to my relief, then turned and headed out the door.

CHAPTER 10

I had planned to spend the remainder of the day, trying to revise for my exams, but my focus kept drifting from school work back to this house and its savage past. I forced myself to keep going until lunch, although I was doubtful any of it was sinking in.

After lunch, I started to browse the internet. I wasn't really sure what I was looking for; however, I did discover that Jem's grandfather, Derek Trerise, had called the police on the night of the last murder, when he was woken up by the sound of gunshots.

Switching off my computer, I leant back in my chair and gazed out over the yard. This house and its past were driving me insane. Every minute of the day, it ate away at me. I knew it was silly, knew that I should be focusing on revising for my exams, but I just longed to know more.

Thoughts of my mum kept running through my mind. Could her fear of the house really be due to the fact that her family had been murdered here? I tried to imagine what that would be like and wondered if I would feel the same, were I in her shoes. Clearly, I would be uneasy; but, I felt certain that my blame would fall on the person and not the house.

Also, her fears seemed to revolve around areas that had no connection to the murders at all. The well, after all, was just a well. Nothing had happened by it or involving it and the same was true of the passage to the den; yet, she had seemed petrified of both, which surely meant mum knew something that I didn't.

I reached for my journal, flicking it open to a fresh page, and tried to think of possible ways to figure out the truth. I jotted down the obvious sources first, which included Mum, Reno(if he was still alive), and Jem's grandfather. I added to this a trip to the library, where I hoped I would have more luck on the newspaper front, and then tried to think of less conventional ways, a psychic medium, perhaps.

As I pondered on this, I remembered a book that I'd read, which I had seen just a few days ago, when I'd been unpacking my stuff.

The book was about Psychometry. It explained that people leave energy on the things around them and that, by touching or holding these objects, you could connect with a person and get a glimpse of some of the more traumatic episodes in their lives.

I had always had an interest in things like that, while maintaining a fair amount of scepticism; however, on trying it out for myself a few times, I had gotten results, at least I had seen things. Although, I had never been sure if it was more a case of an overactive imagination on my part or genuinely what had happened to that object.

But, right now, I was bursting with questions and willing to give anything a try. I jumped up and headed for my bookshelf, tracing a finger along the spines, as I slowly made my way down the shelves. When I found the desired book, I took it across to my bed and curling my legs up underneath me, I began to read.

*

As I looked around me, my eyes fell on the beams and I

instantly remembered something my father had said, when we first moved to Reno, about how the beams in the house had survived intact, since the eighteen hundreds. They were the originals and therefore would have been witness to everything that happened at Insane Reno, the murders included.

I climbed onto my bed and reached up to one of the beams. Placing a hand on either side and closing my eyes, I took a deep breath and tried to clear my mind.

For some time it seemed as if nothing was going to happen. The room remained silent and I was left, feeling like a fool, who was essentially alone in her room, hugging a large wooden beam; but, as I was about to give up hope, I heard a gentle tapping at my bedroom window that steadily grew louder and louder and was followed by a deafening clap of thunder that caused me to jump out of my skin.

Still clutching my eyes tightly closed, I listened to the windows rattle, as if being battered by a heavy storm, and then the light behind my eyelids suddenly flashed bright. I opened my eyes hurriedly and gazed at my room, which was now enveloped in total darkness, the daylight seeming to have evaporated into thin air.

As another thunder clap shook me to my core, I gazed into the blackness, trying to make out my room. It was only when another flash of lightning flooded the small space that I realised my room, although in some ways familiar, was essentially no longer my own; filled instead with someone else's furniture.

I slowly released my grip on the beam and felt the bed, beneath me, begin to wobble violently. As I rested my palms on its surface, I realised that I was, in fact, no longer on my bed, but instead balancing precariously on a child's wooden desk that was clearly not designed to withstand the weight of a slightly bigger than average teenage girl.

Gripping hold of the window sill, in an attempt to take

as much of my weight off the desk as possible, I jumped down, cringing, as I thudded loudly onto the floor.

I waited silently for a few minutes, wishing the storm would quit its angry rambling long enough for me to hear if there was any movement within the dark house. Eventually, I conceded that this was unlikely to happen and, forcing myself to be brave, I made my way towards a small set of shelves, on the wall, opposite, and begin to examine its contents.

There were four shelves; on each of which sat a collection of pristine china dolls in pretty frocks and, as I scanned the shelves, I was aware that I had seen each of these dolls, before, and had hated all of them with a passion.

Then I spotted Abigail, the doll that had gotten me grounded for a month; when I, unable to take her penetrating stare any longer, had stuffed her under the sofa cushion, only for my dad to drop down heavily onto it, after a hard day at work, and shatter Abigail's smug, little face into smithereens. It was safe to say, I was less than pleased to see her resurrected, especially when that resurrection was taking place on a stormy night in my new bedroom.

As another flash of lightning lit up the faces of the dolls and reminded me exactly why I had stuffed Abigail under that cushion, I made a hasty retreat to the other side of the room, where the foot of a small, cast iron bed jutted out from the recess made by the bay window.

Noting that the sheets were flung back, as if the occupant of the bed had left in a hurry, I felt a shiver run down my spine and quickly turned around, heading towards the bedroom door; stopping suddenly, as I spotted a familiar looking box that brought back vivid memories sat atop a small cabinet.

My need to exit this room with its creepy china dolls was quickly replaced by my ever desperate need to disobey my mother. As I reached for the small box and gently lifted the lid, the tiny white ballerina inside sprung up, but failed to start her slow twirl. My mother had idolized this sweet little box and had always forbidden me to touch it; only ever allowing me to watch, as she turned the key and set the ballerina dancing. Now, unable to resist, I reached for the little, silver key and began to turn it steadily, resisting the urge to overwind it and get revenge.

The pretty ballerina started to twirl, as gentle music filled the small room, causing me to forget for a second where I was; then, hearing a floorboard creak outside in the hall, I hurriedly snapped the lid shut, straining my ears, as I tried to make out any further sounds.

When none came, I replaced the box on the dresser and turned, once more, to scan the room; spotting a small book on the floor near the desk, wondering if I had knocked it off, when jumping from there earlier. I tentatively moved towards it, bending down to examine it, as another flash of lightning zigzagged across the sky.

In an instant, my heart leapt into my throat, as I found myself suddenly face to face with a small child; a small child, whose eyes belonged to my mother and who, in every other way, was a younger version of myself.

I stood there, rooted in place, gazing at the little girl, who seemed not to have noticed me. It was clear she was scared; but, as I stood there, unable to move, it became more and more apparent that it was not me that she was afraid of. Growing more confident, I slowly began to reach a hand towards her, wondering if she could see me at all; however, my hand froze mid-way, as a loud bang rang through the house; a bang that, this time, was definitely not thunder.

A woman's scream echoed through the house, but was quickly silenced by a second bang that sent me scrambling under the desk in a panic with this miniature version of myself.

The house that had been silent, just minutes ago, was now filled with pitiful cries, but it was not the little girl, who was crying. She sat under the desk, biting her bottom lip; her eyes clenched shut, hands clamped to her ears, as heavy footsteps crashed around nearby. A loud thud resonated through the house, followed by a piercing scream, which was quickly silenced by a third shot; then all fell silent, once more, as I sat crumpled beneath the tiny desk, my legs pressed up against the little girls, while we both shook with fright.

I heard shuffling footsteps, outside the bedroom door, and waited with baited breath for it to be thrown wide; my heart pounding violently in my chest, as the door handle slowly began to move. I felt nauseous with fear, as I pulled my hands to my chest and sent a silent prayer to God to save both me and the small girl. For once in my life, it seemed he was listening, as suddenly, the handle was released and the heavy steps moved away from the door, hitting the stairs, and descending at speed. A few gentle thuds followed from below, but the cascade of whispered thanks I was sending to God for his hurried intervention were quickly silenced; as, once again, I heard footsteps on the stairs, followed, shortly after, by an animalistic scream of anguish.

Sobs filled the house, once more; this time, loud, deep sobs that made me clamp my hands to my ears, then a deep, yet childish voice calling out, "Tommy," followed by more footsteps, a door creaking, open, and a second, anguished filled, scream.

"Annie," the same voice called, and I watched the little girl look towards the door, then shift slightly, as if she wanted to get up, but was unable to move.

"Annie," the voice called again, sounding closer. A few seconds later the door slowly opened; a head, peering through the gap and, as a flash of lightning lit up the room, I saw the lopsided face of the man that stood there, a gun, clutched in his hands. My breath froze in my throat, once more, as I realised I was now looking at Reno.

"Annie," he called nervously, shuffling into the room, "Annie," again. This time it seemed to catch in his throat, as a sob burst forth, and he dropped with a loud thud, onto his knees. As lightning lit the room, once more, I saw Reno, collapsed on the floor, his head buried in his arms, one hand still tightly clutching the gun.

My attention quickly jumped back to the small figure hiding beside me as she began to move, crawling out from under the desk. My hand instantly shot out to grab for her leg, but simply passed right through it, as she rushed to Reno's side, flinging her arms around him, causing him to cry all the harder.

"Sorry Annie," he cried, dropping the gun, as he sat up and pulled the small girl into his arms.

Reno sounded like a child; as frightened, it seemed, as Annie, and yet this was all his fault, he was the culprit. How could she go to him like that, knowing what he had just done to her family? It didn't make sense.

Hours seemed to pass as I sat there watching Reno rocking backwards and forward and, although my mum was in his arms, it was clear that he was not rocking to sooth her, but for his own needs; fast, jerky movements that could hardly be deemed soothing.

Over and over, he simply said, "Sorry," as if that made everything ok. I was mad; mad at my mum for going to him and mad at him for all the lives he had taken; innocent lives, people who had gone out of their way to help him, when he was no real relation to them.

The storm continued to rage outside; the rain, smashing against the window pane viciously, as if desperate to get in and add to the destruction, and then, through the rain and the thunder, I thought I heard the sound of sirens, faint and distant, but slowly growing louder.

I looked to Reno and Annie, waiting for them to register the sound. Annie was already looking up, but Reno did not move, until the flashing lights began to reflect on the wall of the room and this only caused him to grab for the gun, pulling it tight against him and Annie, before returning to his incessant rocking, as he chanted over and over again, the word, "Sorry."

Soon, I could hear footsteps below, slowly moving from room to room, before coming up the stairs; growing closer and closer, the crackling of radios, echoing through the house, hurried voices whispering, and then the door to the room was flung open. Two officers came in, guns held out in front of them.

"Drop the gun," a large, burly officer yelled, at Reno, who let out an animalistic scream, and clutched Annie tighter to him, "Drop it," the officer yelled again, and I watched, as Annie cuddled tighter into Reno, shaking violently now, her frightened sobs, suddenly filling the room; but still, he would not drop the gun.

"Now!" The officer yelled, and this time Reno let the gun drop. It had barely hit the floor, before the officer was diving onto him, pulling him back onto the floor, while the second officer tried to extract Annie from his arms.

The scene was a mess; Annie screaming with fright. While one officer wrapped his arms around her waist, trying to tug her small body free of Reno's arms, his colleague tried to force Reno to let go.

"No! No! No! Mine! You can't have, no!" Reno whined, as a second set of officers burst into the room, clearly drawn by the commotion.

They both surveyed the scene, then dived for Reno; one of them dropping a knee down onto Reno's chest to pin him in place, while the other savagely pulled out a baton and smashed it down hard, on Reno's left arm.

It had the desired effect and Reno yelled in pain, pulling his arms back into his chest and sending the officer, who had been tugging at Annie, flying backwards into the desk, making me jump out of my skin.

I watched mortified, as Annie kicked out, fighting with all her might to get back to the very man who had murdered her whole family; her feet crashing into the small dresser, by the door, as she sent her small music box flying across the room, the lid opening, and the small ballerina inside, beginning to twirl.

The room was suddenly filled with soft music, while Annie screamed at the top of her lungs and Reno simply laid there, pinned beneath two officers, murmuring, "Sorry," over and over, as the room slowly faded, until all I could hear was swan lake, playing faintly in my head.

*

I was laid on my bed, surrounded by darkness. At first, I thought I was still there, that this was all that was left, just this room and the night; but, as I sat up, I realized I was clutching the book on Psychometry. Reaching for the lamp beside my bed, I flicked it on, gazing about me. Everything was normal; all as it was meant to be. Only the pounding of my heart gave away my recent experience; an experience which I had deemed to be so real, but which now seemed to have been nothing more than a bad dream.

I laid the book on the bed, burying my face in my hands, as I tried to rationalize with myself. It had all seemed so real. I was positive I had stood on the bed and reached for that beam; certain of it. I could still remember the feel of the slightly rough wood, as my hands rested upon it, yet here I was, sat on my bed, the book, still in my hand. I'd not been holding the book, when I'd reached for the beam. I cursed under my breath, shaking my head as, once more, I felt like an idiot; realizing that all I had done was dream up my own imaginings of the happenings that night.

I slid back down my bed, turning onto my side and gazing across the room blankly. Was I losing my mind; becoming as paranoid and neurotic as my mother?

I laid there on my bed, like that, for what felt like hours, trying to make sense of what I had seen, thinking back over everything I had been told. The truth was I had read a book about Psychometry and fallen asleep, only to dream up some twisted nightmare that, undoubtedly, had no real basis in reality and was merely conjured up images, based on how I perceived it to have looked and the people involved to have acted on that terrible night; maybe adding in a few extra details to make the whole scene more exciting.

Although, I considered actually trying out the Psychometry for real, I knew that I just did not trust the process enough to have any faith in it. The idea was nice, the whole trapped energies thing, but the chances of it actually being real and actually working, I personally felt were slim. The only thing I would see, I was sure, was what I had already imagined up in my dream and that was worthless.

I shook my head, hating this house and the way it intrigued me. That intrigue had been there since moving in; but, finding out that my mum was a victim of the horrible crimes committed here had made that intrigue deepen, and now I just had to know the truth; had to figure it all out and make sense of it. I just didn't know how I was going to do that.

My mother was never going to talk, especially not to me, because she never told me anything. News reports might give me a little more information or at least their version of it, but there was no guarantee that these reports would be correct. As mum hadn't talked about it, and it seemed doubtful that Reno would have, in all likeliness, the only thing they would be able to tell me is who died in what room and how they met their end.

Mum seemed the only possible answer, at least for the last set of murders that had taken place here; however, those were not the only murders committed here. There were the earlier ones, too, and I really wanted someone who could shed more light on those, as well.

Jem's grandfather, of course, was the most likely candidate, but I didn't feel confident enough to talk to him. Morwena, though, seemed to have a good bond with her grandfather. Perhaps, if I befriended her or helped her with her course work, I might be able to persuade her to see what her grandfather knows about the house and its history.

Looking at the clock, I saw that it was gone midnight and realized that I must have been asleep for some time. I decided there was little point me getting up now and so simply closed my eyes and allowed myself to drift off to sleep, once more.

CHAPTER 11

The next morning I decided to go for a ride, feeling that time away from the house and some fresh air would do me good and would hopefully help take my mind of things, if only for a little while.

I headed out to the stable, relieved to see no sign of Jem, as I tacked up the fat, little mare that nuzzled continually at my pockets, clearly hoping for a treat. I gently pushed her head away, checked that her lead rope was securely fastened, and headed back into the kitchen to get a pack of spearmint Polo's; a favourite with the horses at the local stables. As I turned to head back outside, I heard a thud that sounded as if it had come from my room, above.

I listened silently for a few moments, but hearing nothing more and not feeling brave enough to investigate, I hurried outside.

Misty greeted me with a happy whinny and stamped her hooves impatiently, as I slipped the bridle over her head. I smiled when she allowed me to slip the bit gently into her mouth without a fuss; something some of the stables horses had never been eager to accept without a fight. Holding my palm out flat, I dropped a couple of Polo's onto it; smiling as she instantly devoured them, then nudged me longingly, hoping for more.

"Hey, you're fat enough as it is, missy," I chided, stashing the packet of mints in my back pocket, "Maybe, if you're good, you can have some more later," I added, leading her out into the yard and lifting my rucksack onto my back, before running my hands affectionately down her neck and along her shoulders.

Gripping the saddle, I eased myself up onto her stout back, clicking my tongue lightly, as I directed her towards the open moors; smiling happily, as the sunshine warmed my skin.

It was a beautiful day and after riding for only a few minutes, I spotted a buzzard, floating gently on the breeze, scanning the ground for a tasty meal.

I glanced back towards the farm, watching it fade slowly into the distance, then frowned, as I thought I saw what looked like a figure, standing at the bay window in my room. Flicking my gaze away hurriedly, I stared ahead, my mind a rush with thoughts; until, at last, I braved a second look.

Gazing at the window, I squinted, as if this would help me make out the figure that was no longer there; which may have, in fact, never have been there at all.

Shaking my head, I laughed, "...keep seeing things that aren't there and people are gonna think you're as nuts as your mum," I said aloud, realising that this was only further proving my insanity. I hurriedly turned my attention back to the buzzard, now slowly gliding above us, watching the ground, as if hoping Misty would scare up something tasty.

It followed us like this for some time, before slowly drifting away on the wind, the sun gleaming on its feathers, as it circled above a patch of ground over to my right; its eyes lighting on something, it stopped and hovered on the spot, for a few seconds, before swooping towards the ground with speed and disappearing from sight in some long grass. When it re-emerged, a short while later, it had a small animal gripped between its talons.

I wondered if the small mammal had been aware that it was being watched; had sensed the looming danger or if it had simply felt the bird's sharp claws pierce its skin, snatching it away to its death, before it had even been aware of its presence. Either way, I prayed that death had been swift and relatively painless for the small animal.

Being watched, I'd felt that way a lot myself lately. I had put it down to the house's past causing me to be paranoid. I had gotten good at making excuses for every thud, creak, and shadow that I was scared by.

I had considered the possibilities, of course, first the obvious one, the house being old, which was one of my favourites; after all, old houses were prone to creaks and drafts were to be expected, right?

It was always small things, the worst having been shadows, which I often saw move past windows or doors late at night when it was quite dark outside. This I passed off as clouds passing over the moon, making the darkness that little bit blacker and it made sense, after all. I had always lived on streets that were well lit by streetlights. Here, on the moors, as soon as the sun disappeared from sight, the farm would be enveloped by the night. The only lights were those that my father had fitted, which were switched on only when one of us needed to head out to the yard.

I'd also considered the possibility that the victims of Reno had remained behind in spirit form, unable to move on due to their brutal exit from this world; but, this too, had scared me, because I was all too aware of the fact that not all spirits were friendly, so I had again flipped back to the old house theory, relying on it to keep me from becoming a nervous wreck, like my mother.

I frowned, realising that I was still letting the house prey on my mind, and silently chastised myself. I was out on a beautiful day, riding on the moors, something that I had always longed to do. I should be enjoying myself, not freaking out over some shadow I'd imagined into a figure in my bedroom window.

Lifting my hand and glancing at my watch, I realised that I had already been riding for almost an hour. Spotting a small stream up ahead, I decided to take a break, turning Misty towards it. I scanned the moorland around me, searching for a nice place to stop and sketch for a while.

I settled on a small, rocky area, close to the stream, where I had spotted a large, flat stone, on which I could sit comfortably.

Dismounting from Misty, I led her to the water, where I watched her drink slowly.

"I'm gonna trust you not to wander, too far," I said to her, nervously, "I'll only ever trust you the once and there's more Polo's in it for you, if you stay close. No Polo's," I added, firmly, "if you make me chase you."

I knew I was taking a risk. I did not know Misty very well, at all, and she had not built up any loyalty towards me. However, my dreams of riding on the moors had included the loyal horse that I could trust to graze nearby, without it wandering, too far away; besides, there was really nothing I could tie her to, so I just had to take the chance and pray that it paid off.

Misty merely flicked her tail lazily at a fly that was buzzing around her rump and then bashed her head against me, as if to say, 'whatever.'

I moved across to the rock, pulling my rucksack, off my back, and took out my sketchpad and pencils. I had wanted to draw the moors, ever since we'd moved to Reno; but had held off, unsure if I was up to the challenge.

It was such a complicated terrain, with so many different hues of green that faded to burnt ambers, golden yellows, and crisp browns. On top of this, the light was ever changing. Horses, sheep, and even cattle, roamed freely and it was such a large, open space that it was going to be hard to pick a specific area and focus on that alone.

I scanned the scene before me and then slipped a pencil out of the pack, determined to give it my best shot.

I lost myself quickly in my work; only being reminded of Misty when, over an hour later, she nudged me in the back, sending a dark line, skidding across the paper.

I scowled, but was silently relieved that she had not run off on me. After all, she could have gone miles in the time I had been lost in my concentration. Bearing in mind that she was not my horse, I was feeling somewhat guilty, for not keeping a closer eye on her.

Deciding there was no point beating myself up over something that had worked out fine on its own, I packed up my stuff and fished the Polo's out of my pocket, heaping praise on Misty, while sending a silent 'thank you' to the heavens.

I put on my rucksack and climbed onto Misty's back, clicking her into a walk. Rubbing one hand lightly down her neck, I leaned forward and whispered in her ear, "You're a good girl, Misty," then gently kicked her into a trot, determined to make it home in time for lunch.

*

Having taken my time to make sure Misty was settled back into her stable, I headed into the farmhouse and glanced around the empty kitchen with disappointment. Glancing at the clock, I saw that it was gone twelve and seeing no mess, I knew that Jem had not yet been there. Wondering where he had got to, I headed out into the yard; checking in the barn, the stable block, the front yard, and lastly, heading into the outbuildings that had been converted for my father's practice.

My father was sat behind the reception desk, surrounded by paperwork, and stabbing angrily at the computer keys. His short, brown hair stuck up, as if he had been electrocuted and I knew that he had been scratching at his head; something my father did furiously, when he was stressed and struggling to figure something out.

"What's the matter dad?" I asked, and frowned, when he didn't even bother to look up; instead, continuing to stab at the keys and tut angrily, while his normally soft, smiling face twisted with frustration.

"I can't figure this stupid program out," he hissed, thumping the computer screen, as if trying to knock some sense into it, "Easy," he spat angrily, "that's what they said on the box; easy setup with simple instructions. Minutes, they claimed it would take. I've been here nearly two hours and I still can't get the stupid thing to work."

"Here let me look," I said, moving around the desk and gazing at the computer screen, on which flashed a message, asking for the patient's name.

"You have to store the patient info, before you can search for it;" I told him, then added, "and seeing you don't have any yet, as you haven't opened, you'll have to make one up to test it."

"That's what I've been doing!" He snapped angrily, and stabbed a name into the little box provided, "It just keeps saying, person not found; but, I'm not trying to find them, I'm trying to add them to it."

"Well, you're in the wrong bit for that," I said smiling, then pointed to the tabs at the top of the screen, "Look, you're in patient info. You need to be in the 'new' tab," I added, taking control of the mouse and clicking the correct tab open, "See? You can put everything in here; new products, new patients, and it makes it easy, too," I said, clicking on the new patient button and then typing in my name and details, in way of demonstration.

My father looked at the screen with a frown, scratched irritably at his head, and said, "Well, why can't they just tell you that?"

"Did you read the instructions?" I asked, picking up

the small booklet and skimming through it, while my father gazed up at me like a naughty little school boy; eyes wide and puppyish.

"It said it was easy," my father said, in way of his defence. I merely shook my head and changed the subject. There was no way I was going to be like my mother and chastise my father for his ignorance.

"Have you seen Jem?" I asked.

"Not for a while. No," he said; his gaze locked on the computer screen, as he flicked through the different tabs, "Last time I saw him, he was yanking out brambles in the front yard. I told him I'd hire someone in to do that, but he insisted. I think he's getting bored, waiting for us to get some livestock in."

I nodded and smiled, "Well he should be doing something. After all, you are paying him."

"Not for dirty jobs like that, though."

"Dad you hired him to run and take care of the farm. Technically any job that needs doing round here should be on Jem's list of 'to do's.' You can't just hire someone else in, whenever you feel bad about getting him to do a job."

"You're right, of course," he said, with a smile, reaching out and taking my hand, "You have a very wise head on those shoulders, just like your mother," he said; those words stinging me to the core. The last thing I wanted was to be anything like my mother, "If I didn't have you, I don't know what I would do," he said, with a sad smile, giving my hand a gentle squeeze.

I leant into him lightly, then and extracting my hand from his, I wrapped my arms around his shoulders.

"I love you, Dad," I said, with a smile.

"Likewise, little girl," he replied, with a laugh, knowing how much I hated him calling me that. Bringing up my hand, I clipped him over the head playfully. My father let out an exasperated grunt and said, "She giveth and then she taketh away," a huge smile, spreading over his face.

I merely rolled my eyes and headed back out to the yard, my father's chuckles, following me to the door.

Heading over to the barn, I gazed up the steps that led to Jem's annex and smiled. He was always so cocky, when it came to meal times; maybe this was my chance to really show him up.

Running back to the kitchen, I hurriedly invaded the cupboards and threw together a ham salad sandwich with mayo, before rushing back out to the yard and up the stairs to Jem's annex.

I peered through the little window in the door, but could not see him in the first room of his little home; however, I could hear him whistling away happily, somewhere inside, and so, I tapped lightly on the door.

The whistling paused briefly and I heard the soft slap of bare feet on bare wood; Jem's face, appearing in the small window, a few minutes later.

"Lunch is served," I called, holding up the sandwich and beaming. If he wanted lunch, he was going to bloody well get it.

He tugged open the door; a towel draped around his middle. I fought not to stare at his taught stomach and heavily defined eight pack and lost. My eyes fixed on his chest, as little droplets of moisture, glistened on his half naked body.

"Lunch…" I managed to mumble, my mind going completely blank. He was a god and as much as I hated to admit it, I could see no flaws in his body or with his looks, anywhere. I just prayed that whatever was hiding beneath that towel was small and shrivelled.

"...is cooking," he said, suddenly and I looked up at him.

"Huh?" I replied, dumbly.

"You said lunch," he replied, "so, I said, is cooking," he added, calmly.

"No. Lunch is cooked," I said, proffering the sandwich.

"That isn't cooked," he replied.

"It's still lunch though, isn't it?"

"You eat it, then," he added, "and I'll enjoy the poached eggs, I just cooked; all to myself."

I loved poached eggs. It was my favourite meal and something my dad used to make for me all the time.

"You're right. Sandwiches suck," I said, and pushed past him; however, his little kitchen, come living room, was bare.

"Where's the food?" I asked, dumbstruck, even opening the microwave to check that it wasn't hidden inside.

"Gotcha!" he said, and scurried through to the other room; yelling over his shoulder, "Now, how about you go cook me a proper lunch, while I get dressed?"

*

I stood in the kitchen, gazing at the cooker with uncertainty. Yes, I had eaten lots of poached eggs; but, I had never made any and I certainly hadn't paid any attention, when my father did.

Cooking had never seemed important to me. There were always easier ways to get food than to cook it and when I did want something cooked, there had always been someone to do it for me. Without mum around, the number of people had gone down and to be fair, dad was so busy trying to set up his practice that I was lucky to see him more than a couple of hours a day. Until now, Jem had been cooking, so it hadn't been a problem; however, Jem was starting to make me question my inability to cook and, as much as I hated to admit it, I longed to impress him.

I was also beginning to realise that my parents had protected me in more ways than one; because, unlike Morwena, I had never had to do chores, had never been forced to get up before I was ready, and had been encouraged to do what I wanted at all times.

It was only now, with mum gone, that I was beginning to realise how much she had done. Although, the kitchen was relatively tidy, there were still the unmistakable signs of grime, showing. The worktop was grubby, the floor was coated in a dusting of dried dirt traipsed in from the yard, and there was a heap of dirty washing in the utility.

In the cottage, there had never been even a speck of dirt and certainly never any dirty laundry.

I walked through to the living room and frowned. This was even worse; dirty mugs and ring marks on the coffee table, discarded books and magazines, and a cluster of my father's paperwork, scattered across his desk, in the foot of the L, in a disorganised mess.

I shuffled together his papers and stacked them neatly, then gathered up the coffee cups and headed for the kitchen. I couldn't cook, but I could pull my weight, in other ways.

Returning to the living room, I gathered together the collection of books and headed through to the den; pausing at the door, certain I could hear muffled voices coming from inside. I tapped lightly, in case my father was in there with someone, but there was no response, so I gently eased the door open.

The room was empty, but the voices stopped instantly; as if I had, in fact, interrupted a private conversation. I shook it off, certain I was imagining things, and began to slowly stack the books on the shelf.

For the first time, I felt unnerved in this tiny room, as if someone was watching me; a feeling I had felt a few times in other areas of the house.

Once the books were all neatly put away, I headed for the door; pausing, once I had stepped through it, to glance back at the empty room. It was still and quiet. Shrugging, I pulled the door to and, as soon as the latch clicked shut, the voices started, once more.

I was frozen to the spot, straining my ears to work out the words, but it was no good. I took a deep breath, grabbed the latch, and threw the door wide. Once again, the voices stopped instantly, but there was definitely no one in the room.

"Hello," I called, nervously, "is someone there?" There was no response; nothing, just dead silence, but I was positive that I had not imagined the voices. Closing the door, I rushed down the passage, back to the kitchen.

I tried to reassure myself that they were only voices. People murdered often couldn't move on. There were bound to be ghosts in this house. Chances were they were nice ghosts, the victims, not the murderer; but, suddenly I had one question I needed answered, more than any other. Was Reno still alive and, if not, would he have come back to haunt the house he had murdered for?

CHAPTER 12

When Jem walked into the kitchen, I was down on the floor, scrubbing a stubborn stain, my I-pod on full blast, determined to block out the voices that had refused to stop echoing from the den.

My nerves were completely on edge by this point, and when Jem tapped me lightly on the shoulder I screamed, jumping up with arms outstretched, prepared to defend myself.

"Whoa!" Jem cried, his hands shooting up in mock surrender, then quickly lowering them, once more, at the sight of the tears, now trickling down my face, "Tiz, what's the matter?" He asked, his voice full of concern.

I yanked out my earphones, then held a hand up to silence Jem, as I listened for the voices; which, to my relief, seemed to have ceased their endless chatter.

Turning to look at Jem, once more, I snapped, "You don't frigging sneak up on people! What did you think I'd do, roll over and ask you to scratch my belly?" I snarled. There was no way I was telling him what I'd heard.

"Sorry," he said, eyeing me with concern, "Are you sure you're ok?"

"Fine!" I snapped, throwing the sponge in the bucket, and stormed from the room, unable to cope with him any longer.

*

I sat in my room for half an hour, gazing dumbly out across the moors. I just couldn't shake my unease; despite Jem's whistling, which carried to me from the kitchen below and reassured me that I was no longer alone.

I dug in my pocket and pulled out my phone, gazing at the screen with uncertainty. I'd never gone to my mum for anything, but I had to know more about this house, had to get some answers.

Her fear of this place had been so intense that I was sure, if nothing else, she would believe me about the voices; however, I struggled to hold a conversation with my mother that didn't end up with me screaming at her in a rage and so it was several minutes before I was able to bite the bullet and dial her number.

Mum answered on the second ring, "The Bray household, how may I help you?" She asked in her posh telephone voice.

"Mum?" I said weakly.

"Tizzy!" She said, her voice instantly changing to a softer tone, "How are you? Are you ok? Is something the matter?" She hissed into the phone, seemingly as if she were afraid to be overheard.

"I heard voices in the den," I said, doing my best to ignore her insanity; desperate as I was to get it out.

"They're in the room?" She asked, her voice dropping so low now, I could barely hear her, "I knew they would be; they always are."

"But, there wasn't anyone in there," I said, "I checked it twice; but, as soon as I opened the door, the voices stopped."

"Of course they did, Tizzy. They don't want you to find them. It's a secret, isn't it?" She hissed, as if I was an idiot.

"Tell your dad. Tell him to bring you home. It isn't safe

there, Tizzy. They're still doing it; you have to get out."

"Who is?" I hissed, desperate for her to just explain things for once, "Mum, did they do this while you were here? Did you hear the voices?" I asked.

"Come back to Bude, Tizzy," she replied, simply, "We shouldn't be talking about this on the phone, it isn't safe. Please, I love you, I'm worried about you, and I just need you home with me," she cried, before adding, "I have to go now, but please just think it over and I promise, if you come back for good, I'll explain everything, ok?" And, with that, I heard a click and the line went dead.

I cursed under my breath. Why did she have to be such a drama queen? Why couldn't she just be straight with me and tell me the truth?

I was certain she must have heard the voices, too, when she had lived here; but, I hated to assume anything, and she was refusing to give me hard facts.

I pulled out my journal and jotted down the happenings of the morning; noting that it had gone quiet downstairs. I guessed that lunch was ready and although I knew there would be a plate of food waiting for me, the conversation with my mother had seriously diminished my appetite. I continued to write; glancing up only when I heard the double doors below, close.

I looked out of my window and across the yard, where I could see Jem, heading for the barn. A wave of unease instantly washed over me at the thought of being alone in the house again, but I brushed it aside, burying my head back in my journal, determined not to let this house intimidate me any further.

I wrote, undisturbed, for another half an hour, jotting down every thought, question, and possibility that was invading my mind. I became so lost in my work that it took a moment for me to register the soft, rhythmic thud that was echoing through my room; seemingly coming from the wall behind my headboard.

It sounded as if someone was throwing a ball against the wall repeatedly, just a slow, steady, thud, thud, thud, perfectly timed and in rhythm.

I looked up, eyes wide, and gazed at the wall, but there was nothing there; yet the sound continued, thud, thud, thud.

I stood up and slowly moved down the room, resting a hand lightly on the wall, just to the side of the thud, but there was nothing, no movement or vibration. But then, why would there be? The walls in this house, even the dividing walls, were pretty thick.

Feeling more confident, I climbed onto the bed and instantly felt a drop in temperature that sent a shiver running through me. Cold spots; I'd read enough ghost books to know that colds spots were a common occurrence, believed to be connected with the presence of spirits.

I reached out, this time placing my hand on the wall above my headboard and actually felt the wall quiver, as the invisible object thudded against it. I sat back quickly, confused.

"Is there someone there?" I called, and then waited. I did not have to wait long, as the sound of a child laughing echoed through the wall.

I gasped, crawling back on the bed, my head awash with confusion. I tried to think back to all the shows I'd watched on ghost hunting; tried to remember the sort of things they asked, or did, and again there was the thud, thud, thud, never-ending.

"Are you Tom?" I asked, "Can you make the bang stop if you're Tom?" Instantly, the thudding stopped and I held my breath with fright. Every muscle tensed, as I waited; then the thudding started again, exactly as before, thud, thud, thud.

"Did Reno kill you, Tom?" I asked, not sure what else to do, and, once more, the thudding stopped for a few moments and then continued.

"Are you scared to leave here?" I asked. This time the thudding did not stop, but continued rhythmically.

"Is there anyone else here, any other spirits?" I asked, and the thudding stopped, once more.

"Is Reno's spirit here?" I asked, but there was no pause.

"Am I losing my mind?" I said aloud, and then froze as the thuds stopped. My heart beat echoed in my ears, as I waited for them to begin, once more; but there was nothing, just silence. Shaking, I hurried to my feet and rushed to the bathroom, where I instantly threw up.

Sitting on the bathroom floor, I shook with fright; everything my mother had said, running through my head. I had thought my mum insane; had assumed she was overreacting, but now, I was not so sure.

Pulling myself to my feet, I hurried into my room. Never taking my eyes off the wall behind my headboard, I pulled the wire, free from my laptop and hurriedly stuffed it into my shoulder bag. I couldn't stay in the room, not right now, but I needed to do some research on haunting. I just prayed that it would help ease my fears and not worsen them.

I rushed down the stairs and out of the front door, pausing to glance at the well, a shiver running through my body. I turned my gaze away and ran out of the little, walled in garden and over to the large oak tree, underneath which my father had placed a picnic table.

Yanking my laptop open and sitting down, I quickly checked to make sure that the wireless signal could reach me here and was relieved to see that it could.

I had to stay calm and rational; after all, not all spirits were evil, most were completely harmless. Even those reported to be really evil often didn't do anything to harm the living. Of course, there were poltergeists that could get quite nasty; but, so far, nothing in the house had tried to hurt me.

I typed 'haunting' into the search engine and clicked on the first link, then began to read.

CHAPTER 13

I sat that night around the table with my father and Jem, eating in silence, while they talked happily amongst themselves.

My head awash with all the things I had read that day on ghosts; how to communicate with them, how to get rid of them, and everything in between. My research had helped to calm me a lot, but I was still nervous about the house, especially the two rooms that, until now, had been my favourites.

I gazed first at my father and then Jem, both of them, so calm and relaxed here; neither afraid nor worried in any way. I envied them. I wished, more than anything, that I could go back to that place.

"Are you ok?" My father asked, interrupting my thoughts.

"Fine," I said, as calmly as I could muster. I did not want to get into a conversation about ghosts with him, when Jem was sat right there, and so I fumbled an excuse, "Just worried about my exams, I guess," I lied.

"You'll do fine. I know you need some pretty intense grades to go to veterinary school; but you're smart. If anyone can do it Tiz, you can," he said, confidently.

I shrugged my shoulders and, once again, began to eat. I could feel Jem's eyes on me; boring into the top of my head, but I refused to look up.

*

After dinner, I had headed straight to my room, where I forced myself to lay on my bed. I would not be scared away by some stupid ghosts; assuming, of course, that was what I had even heard. Surely, there had to be a rational explanation.

I knew the chimneys were behind that wall. Perhaps a bird had got stuck down one and had been bashing around, trying to get out. The silences to my questions, simply the bird, pausing to regain its energy.

Ok, so probably not, but there was bound to be a rational explanation. The voices and the child's laughter that I had heard, well, that could simply have been my imagination, playing tricks on me; after all, I was tense.

I jumped, as I heard someone or something rap on my bedroom door. Nervously, I headed towards it on tiptoes, listening for any sound outside. Reaching for the handle, I yanked it open, relief, washing over me when I saw Jem, standing in the doorway; but, seeing his arms folded across his chest, I instantly grew defensive, certain he was here to interfere, in some way.

"What?" I snapped.

"Exam worries, my ass!" Was all Jem said, as he pushed past me, "What's going on Tiz? I mean, earlier on, you practically had a fit when I tapped you on the shoulder. Now, granted, you didn't hear me; but still, you don't freak out like that over being surprised, then at dinner you barely said a word and you sat out on that bench all day, tapping away on your laptop, and, even then, you were on edge. I watched you. I saw you spin round, every time I made a noise; so, fess up, what's going on?"

"Nothing!" I snarled. There was no way I was going to tell him about the things I had heard. The last thing he needed was more ammo for mocking me.

"I guess this house freaks you out; hell, if I'm honest, it does me a tad, but it wasn't bothering you yesterday, so why the sudden change?"

I opened my mouth to speak and then froze, as I saw, out of the window, behind Jem, a deathly white figure with an eerie, blue glow, standing beside a tree, far out on the moors. I closed my eyes, shaking my head, and looked again; but it was gone.

"Just get out and leave me alone!" I snapped, charging at Jem and gripping hold of his arm. He didn't fight me; simply allowed himself to be dragged.

"Tiz, I know I take the piss and shit, but it's just a laugh, I don't mean anything by it, so don't shut me out. If you need someone to talk to, you know where I am."

"Ok," I said, willing to say anything just to get him the hell out of there, and, with that, I pushed him through the door, closing it tightly behind him and collapsing against it.

I gazed down at the floor, not wanting to go back to the window, scared of what I would see; but, in the end, my curiosity got the better of me.

Gazing out to the tree, then all around it, I let out a sigh. There was nothing there. All was still and quiet.

CHAPTER 14

I awoke the next morning after a restless night; having been woken up, more than once, by my own paranoia, and twice, by the thudding on the wall, above my head.

I clambered out from under my quilt and headed for the bathroom; hoping a shower would help wake me up a bit.

I returned to my room half an hour later, somewhat refreshed, and gathered my things together, before heading downstairs, where I could already hear Jem whistling away happily.

As I entered the kitchen, Jem looked up and smiled at me, "Your dad's gone into town and won't be back till this evening. He's set the date for the grand opening, as well, but I'll let him tell you about that," he said with a smile, then added, "How did you sleep?"

"Fine," I lied.

"Morwena called a minute ago; said you can collect your pup today," he continued, piquing my interest, "I told her we'd be there around midday; figured I could take you into town first and get some bits and pieces for it."

I smiled at this, deciding he wasn't a bad guy, really.

"Jem," I said, taking a seat at the table, "your granddad's been looking after this house for years, hasn't he?" I asked.

"Yep," he replied.

"Did he talk about the house much?"

"Not really. I mean he told us about its history and a little about the people that used to live here, but never really talked about the murders or anything. I guess it was almost as painful for him as it is for your mother; after all, he worked for most of the families that were killed and was good friends with the rest. He says it was used for smuggling, but he's always liked to tease people and, personally, I think it's too far back on the moors for that.

He also said it was built by a member of our family; the one that built your room as a shrine for his daughter. That, I think, is true; because my granddad has lots of old journals written by the guy, although we have never been allowed to read them. The problem is it's hard to know with my granddad what is the truth and what's a trick. He has big ideas and big dreams, and this farm, I think, has always felt like home to him, I know he'd love to own it, one day, but I can't see that ever happening.

"So, you don't know much about the murders that took place here, then; I mean other than the most recent?"

"Not really, just the usual rumours. I used to use it as a popularity tool, when I was younger," he said, with a smile, "Wind people up, ya know; tell 'em the place was haunted and make up stories of phantoms and screaming women dressed in white, but really there was never any of that. Shame though, 'cause I like all that sort of stuff. I go every year up to Rough Tor on the anniversary of Charlotte Dymond's murder; just in case, ya know, and that's pretty active. Always get lots of orbs on camera."

"So, you don't think this house is haunted, then?" I asked.

"Not that I've ever seen; although, to be fair, we weren't in here much. Gramps said it was disrespectful to the dead, us kids running around in here; which, of course, back then, I was, and well, once I was older, there wasn't any real reason for me to come here. I guess it had just stopped intriguing me by then."

"What if I told you that there'd been some strange stuff happening?" I asked.

He looked at me then, before quickly turning the hob down and coming across to the table. Flipping one of the chairs round to face him, he sat down, resting his arms on the back, "Like what?" He asked.

"Well..," I said, then paused, worried he would think I had lost the plot. Taking a deep breath I forced myself to continue, "...like yesterday, before you came in and scared me, I was clearing up a bit and heard voices coming from the den; but, when I opened the door, they stopped, so I left, then tried again, and again, they stopped, but there was no one in the room. That's why I had my I-Pod on so loud, to block out the sound," I said.

"And that's why you freaked out so much, when I tapped you on the shoulder?" He added, and I nodded.

"But, that's not all," I said, pausing, as he held up his hand and rushed to the stove. I watched, as he dished up an omelette, splitting it in half and sliding it onto plates, then he returned to the table, handing one of the plates to me, while he flipped his chair back round and signalled for me to go on, "Well, I was in my room and I started hearing this thudding noise; sounded like someone throwing a ball up against the wall, over and over, and when I put my hand on the wall behind my bed, I could feel it vibrating."

"Shit!" He said, then gazed at me, waiting for more.

"Well, I know they ask questions of spirits on them ghost investigation shows and so I asked it to stop making the noise, if the answer was yes to a question, then I asked it a few questions, like was it Tom, my mum's brother, and, you know, just stuff," I added. There was no way I was telling him about it answering yes, when I'd asked if I was going insane, "Well, it said yes to the Tom thing, I mean, the sound stopped, and paused for a while, you know, before it started going again, and last night, I was woken up by the same thudding a couple of times; also, when I was talking to you last night, after you pushed your way into my room, I swear I saw a blue, glowing figure out on the moors. That's part of why I freaked out," I said, then waited for him to finish chewing his food and respond.

"Well, they say ghosts have unfinished business, don't they? Maybe you and your dad moving in triggered them off; plus, if it was your mum's little brother, then maybe he thought you were your mum. I mean, do you look like she did, when she was younger?"

"I dunno. Dad says I do, but I've never seen any photos of her, when she was my age. Dad said she always avoided being in any of his family's pictures; up until they were married, at any rate. I guess she felt she didn't really belong or something."

Jem nodded thoughtfully and chewed on a forkful of omelette, for a few moments, before resting his knife and fork on his plate, "I wouldn't be afraid of this stuff, though, Tiz," he said, "Most ghosts don't actually hurt people. Some give off a bad vibe; but, for the most part, even the bad one's seem to be more of an irritant than a danger."

I nodded weakly, hoping he was right.

"But, you know, if you ever get really worried, just come get me," he added, "If nothing else, I can keep you company and at least try to take your mind off it a bit."

I smiled at this; I was always game for Jem's company and the thought of him actually wanting to offer it was a nice one.

"You should eat up," he said, indicating my food, "Omelettes aren't so nice cold," he added, with a smile.

"So, you don't think I'm nuts, then?" I asked, needing the reassurance.

"God no, Tiz. Shit like this happens. The people that

say ghosts don't exist are nuts. I mean, sure, there are people who claim they've seen stuff they ain't; but, I saw how upset you were yesterday and, well, what I've seen of you so far, you don't seem the sort of person to get frightened over nothing. I'm just glad you decided to talk to me. At least now, I know what's up and can be there, even if there ain't much I can do to stop it; unless, of course, you want me to try and find out about exorcism."

"Do you think that would help?" I asked.

"Maybe, but the way I see it, if a spirit has unfinished business, then maybe it's better to find out what that is, instead of just sending 'em packing. Maybe we should try using a Ouija board or something."

"Aren't they meant to be dangerous?" I asked, shocked.

"Well, yeah, if you summon dark spirits; but, technically, we're only going to be trying to communicate with what's already here and, well, if it's already here, then it can hurt you, whether you use a Ouija board or not, right?"

"I guess," I replied; although, I was not altogether convinced.

CHAPTER 15

When we pulled into the Trerise farm, around midday, Morwena was already waiting with my beautiful puppy in her arms and two adult collies by her side.

"I thought you would want to meet mum and dad," she said, as soon as I stepped from the truck. Indicating the black and white collie, on her left hand side, she added, "This is Sweep," then pointing to the tri-coloured collie, now bouncing around me excitedly, she said, "and that is Beans."

I smiled happily, bending down to make a fuss of Beans, who collapsed onto his side and exposed his belly; his sad, sorrowful eyes gazing up at me and making my heart melt.

"That's Jem's dog," Morwena said, as I pandered to Beans wishes, "He is the perfect example of how not to train a collie," she added, with a laugh.

"Hey, ain't nothing wrong with Beans," Jem said, then whistled, causing Beans to squiggle onto his feet and fly at Jem; jumping right into his arms.

"Oh no, nothing wrong with him at all; at least, not if you like your sheepdog to spend his life on his back, begging for belly rubs."

"Which, I do," Jem replied, happily, placing Beans on the floor and heading into the house; his dog plastered to his heel.

I hurried over to Morwena, giving Sweep an affectionate hug, then turned to my beautiful puppy and gently rubbed my nose against his.

"Mother him like that and you'll have another Beans on your hands." Morwena laughed, handing the squiggling puppy to me.

"Do you go back to school next week, like me?" Morwena asked, and I nodded, "Sucks don't it? All they do is go on and on about our exams and how we gotta work hard and study hard. I swear they just want to sap every ounce of fun out of our lives," she continued.

"If you want good grades, then you have to put in the work," I said, and then, feeling stupid, I hurriedly added, "Sorry, exams are a bit of a bug bear with me at the moment. I want to be a vet, so I have to get really good grades, but I haven't been studying as much as I should, which has left me in a bit of a panic and means the mere mention of them sends me on the defensive."

She nodded knowingly, then said, "I'm not bothered what I get. I'm gonna be a singer and you don't need anything but a good voice and determination for that; but try telling that to mum. She is on at me 24/7 to study this and study that. It's driving me mad."

"Well you could always come round mine if you need a break," I said, seeing my opportunity to talk with Morwena, alone, "Just tell your mum that we're going to study, then we could go for a ride, or walk, or something," I said.

"Hey, that's not a bad idea. What you doing this afternoon?" She asked.

"Nothing; as far as I know," I replied, transferring the pup to my left arm, so I could fish my mobile out of my pocket.

Morwena hurriedly followed suit and we exchanged numbers.

"I'll give you a call before I come and we can go riding over the moors. It's the perfect day for it," she said, happily, "I know all the best spots round here. Maybe I could even get mum to put a picnic together for us," she added.

"Won't that kind of give us away?"

"Nah, I'll just say we're gonna find a quiet spot to work, out in the sun. She won't think nothing of it," she replied.

I smiled, happily, then looked up, as I saw Jem coming out of the house; a tatty dog bed under one arm and a couple of large, metal dog dishes, gripped between his fingers.

"You taking Beans?" Morwena asked.

"Yep," Jem replied.

"But, I wanted him for when the other pups are collected," she added.

"Why, they saw him when they came to choose, didn't they?"

"Well yeah, but still..."

Jem looked down at Beans, still firmly locked to his heel, then shrugged, "Well, give us a call, when all the pups have been collected, and I'll come get him," he said, then headed over to the back of the truck, where Beans' belongings were deposited with a clatter. "I'll come and get you later, dude," he said, rubbing his beautiful collie behind the ear affectionately, before giving him a firm pat on the back and adding, "Go on then, clear off mate."

I smiled, as Beans charged off across the yard with his tail in the air. Spotting one of the Jack Russell's, he set off in a playful game of chase.

"Right, let's get home and get this pup settled in," Jem said; then, looking up at the sound of a car, he turned to Morwena and said, "Looks like people are starting to arrive to get their pups."

Morwena simply smiled, before rushing to greet the

new arrivals; waving a hurried goodbye to me and Jem, as she went.

"Come here," he said, once she was out of earshot, and I moved around the truck to see what he was doing.

I watched him lift up the blanket that was tucked inside the scruffy dog bed, then looked up at him perplexed.

"Where did you get that?" I cried. He pressed his finger to his lips; quickly shushing me.

"My brother, Tristan; only he don't know I got it. He's a fruit loop; what can I say. Anyway, I figure we could use it to try and talk to these ghosts, back at yours," he said, while I gazed at the Ouija board, suddenly feeling very sick.

CHAPTER 16

"What if dad comes in?" I asked, as Jem began to set up the board on the kitchen table.

"He said he'd be gone all day. Even if he does, we can tell him we were just messing around."

"Isn't it meant to be dark, when you do this?" I asked, not that I wanted to do it in the dark; but, right now, I just wanted to stall.

"Just go set up the crate. Pop that pup in with some grub and get your butt back over here," he said.

I groaned, but hurried to do what he asked; setting up the new dog crate, beside the huge inglenook fireplace. The whole time Bailey, as I had decided to call my new pup, bounced around me, trying to see what I was doing.

The crate was huge, but Jem had assured me that it made more sense to get a large one, ready for when Bailey was grown up, so that we would not have to spend more money, later.

Once the crate was up, I placed the soft, chocolate coloured bed I had bought, along with some soft dog toys, at the back of the crate, then laid one of the puppy pads, near the front for easy removal and carefully filled the bowls; one with biscuits, the other with fresh water, and clipped them to the side of the crate.

Happy that Bailey had everything he needed; I slipped

him inside and eased the door gently closed. He dived into his food instantly, completely oblivious to me, as I headed back to the table, where Jem was already sat, waiting for me; the Ouija board, laid out in front of him.

"Are you sure this is a good idea?" I asked.

"Don't worry, it'll be fine," he replied calmly, indicating for me to sit beside him, on the long bench, "Now, I'm not a hundred percent sure how this works, but I think we just put our hands on this thing here and ask questions," he said, taking my hand and folding my fingers until just my index was extended, "Now, you just put that here and I do the same," he said, with a smile, "...and then I guess we ask it something."

Just then, there was a loud rap at the front door, making both Jem and I jump. I laughed nervously, getting to my feet. Thankful for the escape this unexpected visitor was offering, I headed for the front door.

I gazed out through the small window and saw Jem's grandfather and a tall, dark haired guy with hard, sharp eyes, gazing back at me.

"Hi," I said, pulling the door open. I gasped, as the tall guy charged straight in, ignoring me completely, and headed for the kitchen, while Jem's grandfather gently eased past me and smiled.

"Don't mind him; he's just a little disappointed in Jem for taking his stuff." The old man said, then followed after who I now assumed was Tristan.

I hurried behind the grandfather, weaving slightly, and silently urging him to pick up speed, as the sound of yelling reached my ears.

When, at last, Jem's grandfather had passed through the kitchen door, I rushed around him, heading for the dog crate; glancing nervously at the two brothers, who were looking close to punching each other.

I scooped Bailey out and cuddled him close; hoping the racket was not scaring him, too much.

Dad had always told me it was important for animals that were in a new and frightening place not to be stressed out. Bearing this in mind, I hurried from the kitchen and out into the yard. Looking around, I headed for the picnic bench and sat down to wait; soothing Bailey softly.

It seemed an age, before Jem appeared in the yard and waved me over.

"Is everything ok?" I asked.

"Don't mind Tristan. He's a miserable bastard; however, today he has decided to be helpful. He and gramps are going to do the Ouija board with us."

I rolled my eyes. How could he think that was a good outcome? A good outcome would be them snatching the board away; never to be seen again.

Once Bailey was safely sat back in his crate, and we were all gathered around the table, Tristan began.

"First of all, we have to warm the planchette up," he said.

Jem and I both looked at him perplexed.

"The little heart-shaped block that we all have our fingers on," he added, rolling his dark eyes, "For idiot's sake, let's just call it the pointer, ok?" He said, and this time it was Jem and I who rolled our eyes.

"Ok, so we all place our index fingers on the pointer," he continued, emphasising the last word, "We then move the pointer in circular motions around the board for a while to allow it to warm up."

The pointer he was referring to was a small, heart-shaped block of wood with a hole in the centre. This was resting on top of a large wooden board, which had the alphabet, arching across the top in two rows; a 'yes' in the upper left hand corner and a 'no' in the upper right, and finally, a big 'goodbye' scrawled across the bottom.

"Like this," he added, extending his long index finger and placing it lightly on the pointer.

We all followed suit, and then looked to him for

further guidance.

"Now, we start it moving in a circle on the board. Bear in mind, this might not work, being that it is daylight and most recommend this be done at night," he added calmly; and so, we set the little wooden heart circling over the board. Once we had performed four or five circuits, Tristan held up his free hand as a signal to stop.

"Ok, now we start. You must be quiet and just let me do the talking," he said, ignoring, or not seeing, Jem's sulky expression, "Ok, we invite any spirits present here today to communicate with us via this board. We ask that no evil spirits enter the board for they are not welcome."

"Do you hear that?" Jem said, suddenly making me jump.

"Hear what?" Tristan hissed.

"All the evil ghosts, talking amongst themselves. What was that they just said? Hang on. Oh; ok, now I hear them. They're saying 'Fuck! We'd better not go near that board, because we're not welcome'," he said, bursting into laughter.

"Oh, very funny." Tristan hissed.

"Well, seriously dude, do you really think a big, bad ghost is not going to come and talk, simply because you say he isn't welcome?"

"Moving on..." Tristan said, shrugging Jem off, "Is there anyone here with us; anyone at all, here, in this house?" I watched the little heart, my breath frozen in my lungs.

"If there is someone here, please move the pointer to the yes."

Slowly, the pointer began to move towards the upper left hand corner, finally stopping at the yes for a few moments, before returning to the middle.

We all looked up at each other; Jem's eyes, joyful, Tristan's, smug, and the grandfather's, bored.

"Were you one of the people killed here?" Tristan

asked.

Again, the little heart moved to the yes, pausing briefly, before returning to the centre.

"What is your name?" Tristan asked. Slowly the heart began to circle, tiny little spirals all over the board until, at last, it came to rest on the T; pausing, only for a few seconds, before moving to the O, and then to the M, where it stopped completely.

"Tom?" Tristan asked, and the heart moved slowly to the yes.

"Tom, why are you still here? What is stopping you from moving on to the other side?" Tristan asked, and the little heart slowly began to move; and, as it did, Tristan silently urged us, one at a time, to lift our fingers, off the heart.

I was horrified, once we all had; because, not once, had the pointer slowed or stopped, during the process, meaning that the small comfort I had of believing that someone was controlling it was gone and worse yet, when the pointer stopped, the message it had spelled out, was...

'I want you out. They want you dead.'

CHAPTER 17

I sat in my room; Tristan's arm, draped around my shoulders, relieved by the comfort it gave.

"Don't worry about it," he said, for the third time, "What is said on the Ouija board isn't always true. We could have just picked up a bad energy that wanted to scare you," he added, as his hand gently rubbed my arm, in way of reassurance, "Spirits can lie; just like people, and often do. The thing to remember is that most ghosts don't actually hurt people."

"But, some do, right?" I said.

"Yes, they do," he replied, "I was meant to tell you, Morwena won't be coming over today. Mum didn't buy the whole study thing and Morwena is hard at it, in her room," he said, clearly trying to change the subject.

I was partly relieved. All this stuff had spooked me out and I was not feeling in the most sociable mood and neither did it seem, was Jem; who was standing over by my desk with a sulky expression on his face.

"I would just forget all about what happened with the Ouija board and just do something fun. Do you know how to ride a horse?" Tristan asked.

I nodded, noticing that Jem was now glaring at his brother angrily.

"I think Tiz has some revision of her own to do," Jem

interjected, and then glanced at me pleadingly.

"Yeah, I do; plus, I couldn't go off and leave Bailey, not on his first day here," I said, knowing that I had, in fact, planned to do just that with Morwena, but hoping that he'd not been fully aware of the plans his sister and I had made.

"Well, maybe some other time," he replied, and I smiled, looking over at Jem, who seemed happier now.

I wasn't sure why I'd gone along with him. I told myself it was because I was tired and couldn't deal with talking to people right now and I guess, in part, that was true.

"Yeah, that would be nice," I replied, smiling weakly.

"Great," he said, getting to his feet, "Well, I should head off," he added, as Jem rushed for my bedroom door and yanked it open.

"Don't let the door hit you on the way out, bro," he said, and as soon as Tristan had stepped out of the room, Jem slammed the door shut and came to sit beside me, "You ok?" He asked, as I listened to Tristan's footsteps, receding.

"What do you think?" I snapped, "I just had a ghost tell me that it wanted me out and that it wanted me dead; so, yeah, I'm just grand."

"It said you. You could have been anyone. In fact, I bet it was Tristan it was on about, 'cause no one likes him and I mean no one," he joked.

"This isn't funny. I didn't want to do that stupid board in the first place; but, I went along with it because I'm a stupid idiot, and later tonight, I have to go to sleep in a house, full of ghosts that apparently want me dead. What a comforting thought that is."

"Well, you can always come kip on my sofa," he replied, "It's small, but it's pretty comfortable and hell, if you play your cards right, I might even let you share my bed."

I glared at him, then. Why did he have to turn everything into a joke? I was starting to wish I'd taken Tristan up on his offer. At least, he'd actually been trying to put me at ease.

As if he had been reading my mind, Jem suddenly draped an arm around me and smiled, "Look, if you're really worried, just say, and I'll sneak up, after your dad's gone to bed, and kip on the floor."

"Really?" I asked.

"Sure," he replied, then got to his feet, dragging me up with him, "but for now, you're coming downstairs and you're going to learn to cook."

"Oh no!" I cried, "I told you I don't cook."

"Well, you're about to learn," he replied, with a smile.

*

Half an hour later, I was stood in the kitchen, stirring a large pan of minced meat, while Jem leaned against the counter, watching me intently.

"Just make sure you keep stirring, so the mince doesn't stick. I don't want to spend hours, scouring that pan, just because you got lazy," he chirped.

"Oh, so you're doing the dishes, then?" I replied.

"I might, if you don't burn the mince."

He moved around me, slipping a large spoon into the pan of long spaghetti, giving it a gentle stir.

"Ok, now open that jar and pour in the sauce and think yourself lucky, 'cause I'm letting you do this the easy way. If my mum was teaching you, she'd force you to make the sauce, too."

I silently thanked God for this small mercy and then began to tip the sauce into the pan, stirring it vigorously.

"Ok, now turn the heat down and just leave it to simmer, for a while," he added.

"Is that it?" I asked.

He laughed at this, then turned and snatched up the French bread, "It will be, once you chop this up, butter it, drain the pasta, and dish up," he added, smugly.

"What now, Tiz?" He asked, when I rolled my eyes.

"I was just wondering why I have to do everything, when you just seem to be standing there," I replied, then snatching the tea towel off his shoulder, I added, "Maybe you need whipping into shape, too."

"Kinky," he replied, as I spun the tea towel, then flicked it playfully at his hip.

"Should I start preparing for grandchildren?" My father asked, walking into the room; then, spotting Bailey in his crate, he beamed.

"As if," I hissed, stepping away from Jem to go and introduce dad to Bailey.

"Hey, not so fast," Jem said, waving the French stick at me.

"His name's Bailey," I called to dad, as I grudgingly snatched the French stick and started cutting.

CHAPTER 18

I sat out in dad's new surgery, holding Bailey on the examination table, while dad finished checking him over.

"He's a nice healthy pup, Tiz; you picked well," my father said, as he checked Bailey's teeth, "I figured it was about time you got to have a dog. You've wanted one for so long. Just don't let spending time with this one get in the way of your studies. You need really good results to be a vet and you know Jem and I will give him plenty of attention, when you can't," he added, and smiled.

"Did you see mum today?" I asked, changing the subject.

"I did, yeah."

"How is she?"

"Concerned; it seems she had a call from you about hearing voices or something. She wants you to go and live with her."

"I can't. I have to be here with..," he stopped me, mid flow.

"She said Bailey could come, too. I think she just wants you with her, Tiz."

"Do you want me to go?" I cried. He was certainly making it sound like he did.

"Tiz, that is the last thing I want, but I do want you to be happy, and if you would be happier with your mum, then I would be happy for you."

I stood there silent. Part of me did want to get out of this house; especially after everything that had happened, but I couldn't bear the thought of living in a house, without dad.

"I don't want to. If she wants to be where I am, then she'll have to come here," I said with determination, then paused and looked at dad with concern, "Dad, do you really think she will get with Mr Thomas?"

"I think she might. He was in and out today, while I was there and your mum did say that if I needed to sell the cottage, it was alright, as she had somewhere she could go."

My breath caught in my throat at this and anger coursed through my veins. How could she say that to him? She knew he loved her and yet she was just disregarding his feelings, as if they were worthless.

I had once thought that my mum was amazing. I had believed that there was nothing she didn't know about; that she was clever, pretty, and the perfect mum. I had grown up, watching my friend's parents split, and I had been confident that mine would never meet the same fate.

They had been so happy, so in love, and I had always beamed, when people said they were the perfect couple, the couple everyone wanted to be; but, mum had changed all that, had taken all of that away, when she started sniping at dad all the time and then just seemed to ignore us both, whenever possible.

Now, I just hated her. I hated her for taking, what was once the perfect family and crushing it.

I didn't want to be in this house, but I did want to be with dad and I knew that everything was riding on this practice and he needed this house in order to achieve his dream; so, for him, I would stay and I would do my best to make life as easy for him as I could, even if that meant cleaning every day and learning to cook every night.

Placing Bailey gently on the floor, I threw my arms around dad and smiled up at him, "I want to be here with you dad, and the things I heard in the house…well, it was probably just my imagination, playing tricks on me," I said.

He smiled down at me, brushed the hair from my forehead, and kissed me lightly.

"I must have done something right in life," he said, with a smile.

"Why?" I said, knowing full well what his answer would be.

"Because, my darling daughter, someone sent me an angel, straight from heaven, back in '94; a tiny angel, who grew and grew and made my life just perfect," he replied, with a smile.

He had said this to me so many times over the years and it always made me smile; but, my dad was wrong, because I was not the amazing one in this family, he was.

No matter how bad things got, dad was always smiling. Whenever mum or I had been hurt or afraid, dad had been there to comfort us and unlike a lot of men, who put their careers before their family, my father never had.

If I so much as grazed a knee, dad would rush home to see me as soon as he could, and always before he was due to finish work; returning to the surgery, only once he was certain I was happy and my ill's forgotten, in the case of the small ones, and certainly soothed, when things were more serious.

No, I was not an angel; but, I often wondered if my father was.

"You realise," he said, suddenly interrupting my thoughts, "once the surgery is open, you're going to have to keep that pup up off the floor; at least, till he has had all his jabs," he added.

I smiled, "I know dad," I replied, letting go of dad and calling Bailey to me, so that I could give him a hug, "You got your second angel in 2010," I said, with a smile.

"Let's hope your right," he replied, heading across the room and indicating a little, yellow puddle.

I just smiled; handing Bailey to dad, while I went in search of a mop.

CHAPTER 19

I woke up early the next morning and hurriedly threw on my clothes; desperate to get down to the kitchen and see Bailey after the first night in his new home. I had slept reasonably well and there had been no spooky goings on in the night; so, I was feeling pretty good, as I rushed for the door, yanked it open, and then went flying, head first, into the floor.

"Fuck!" I heard Jem cry, and then twisted my head, horrified to see that the large object, I was currently draped over, was him.

"That's nice," he said sarcastically, his head peering out from under a thick blanket, "I sleep outside your door, all night, to protect you from ghosts, and you go and trample all over me," he added.

I gazed at him, shocked; barely able to believe what I was hearing. Sliding off of him and spinning around on my hands and knees to face him, I smiled.

"Have you really been out here, all night?" I asked.

"Pretty much," he replied, with a smile, "So, does that earn me my first breakfast cooked by the ever-radiant Tiz?"

"No," I replied instantly, "but it does earn you this," I added, and bent down; lightly kissing him on the cheek.

"If you give me a grandson, can we call him John?" My

father said, making me fly away from Jem in a flash.

"You can the second one," Jem replied, "but the first one's being named after me," he added.

"I can't believe you just said that!" I cried.

"Who you talking to, your dad or me?" Jem asked.

"Both of you," I hissed, getting to my feet and rushing for the stairs.

"Hey, wait up," Jem called, but I ignored him and barrelled down the stairs.

"Oh, thanks grandpa," I heard him say, "I might have been able to get a real kiss, if you didn't interrupt," he added.

I paused then, waiting for dad's response, and smiled as he said, "You know, as fathers go, I think I'm pretty damn open and pretty damn tolerant and I may not batter an eyelid, when the hired hand sleeps outside my daughter's room or even when he flirts with her incessantly; but, my god, when that man tells me to hold my bladder, so he can get a kiss, well then, that man is pushing his luck."

Men, I would never understand them.

*

I was greeted by both Beans and Bailey, when I entered the kitchen; Beans, rushing over to me and instantly flipping onto his back to beg for a belly rub, while Bailey simply bounced around in his crate excitedly.

"Hello, Beanzifer," I said, giving him a quick pat, "Have you been looking after Bailey for me?" I added, getting back up and moving across to the crate; my smile, quickly turning to a frown, as I saw the mess Bailey had made.

"What have you been doing?" I asked, as I gazed at his shredded puppy pad and the poo that he had smeared on everything; including, I realised, too late, as I lifted him out of the crate, himself.

"Oh my god," I cried, "Bailey what on earth have you been up to?" I added, holding him at arm's length and carrying him up the stairs.

"Whoa! What smells?" Jem asked, still sprawled on the hallway floor.

I held Bailey towards him and watched him wince, "Nice," he said, burying his head beneath his blanket.

I was relieved to find dad had left the bathroom already, and hurriedly placed Bailey in the tub.

Hooking down the shower attachment, I started to run the water; waiting till it was warm, before moving it carefully onto Bailey's tail.

Amazed, when he didn't seem at all fazed, I moved it further up his back; however, this was more than he was prepared to take and instantly he flew into a panic, screaming, as if I had set him on fire.

"I have to wash you, baby. I know you don't like it, but it's for your own good," I called over his screams.

"Sit down," Jem suddenly said from behind me in a calm, but firm, voice and Bailey stopped screaming and just stared at him blankly.

Jem sighed and walked over to the bath, pressed a hand on Bailey's back, and eased him down into a sitting position, "Sit," he said, once Bailey's bottom was firmly down.

"You're gonna have to work on that," he said, taking the shower head from me, "You keep him calm and I'll wash him," he added.

I smiled and did as he said, talking to Bailey softly, while Jem worked; amazed, when Bailey sat there calmly.

"How come he isn't screaming, when you do it?" I asked.

"It's not so much who's washing him, as who is soothing his fears away," Jem replied, with a smile.

Once Bailey was all washed, Jem wrapped him in a towel and began to gently dry him.

"You know, you should probably go get changed," he said, indicating my dressing gown, which was covered in brown paw prints that were definitely not mud; paw prints that had me hurrying from the room, feeling an instant need for a bath, myself.

CHAPTER 20

I worked hard, trying to catch up on my revision, all of that day; stopping every half hour to have a play with Bailey, who, each time, I was relieved to see, had not destroyed his crate.

Jem played on my mind constantly; a smile spreading over my face, every time I thought of him. I had never been the sort of person who got crushes, but I had to admit Jem had wormed his way into my heart. Finding him outside my room this morning and knowing that he had slept on the hard floor all night, to make sure I was ok, had made me go all giddy, inside; not a feeling I was used to.

Noticing Bailey, sniffing around his crate, I hurriedly rushed to get him, running through the house and out into the newly cleared front yard that Jem had been working on for the last few days and placed Bailey down.

This was Bailey's designated safe zone, as my father had called it, and it now had a metal gate, blocking the entrance, so that Bailey could not get out and any dogs that came to visit dad's practice could not get in; at least till Bailey had all his shots, at any rate.

As I watched him nose around in the grass, I smiled. All my life, I had wanted a dog, and although Bailey was already proving to be hard work, I could not be happier.

I lifted my head at the sound of a car approaching and

scowled, when I realised it was Mr Thomas' beloved Triumph Spitfire.

I turned my gaze back to Bailey, who was now crouched down, peeing, and rushed to praise him, silently hoping that, if I pretended they weren't here, they'd go away. No such luck.

I heard the car doors open and close and then a pair of footsteps, heading my way.

"Lizzy," Imelda said, making me jump.

"Hello, Lizzy," her father added, also.

I just gazed at them both blankly; him, short and fat, with little round glasses and balding top, and her, with her perfectly blonde hair and pretty little dress and I wanted to puke.

"Your mum asked me to come talk to you," Mr Thomas said, "She's concerned for your welfare, here."

"I'm with my dad; I'm fine," I replied, as calmly as I could.

"Yes and your dad's a good man, dear; but, it's not your father that your mother is concerned about. Your mum and I..," he began, but stopped, "Your mum would like you to come home."

"I am home," I said.

"Well, we were hoping you would come back to the cottage. What I mean is, your mum is hoping you'll come back," he added.

My father hadn't even been out of the picture a month and this man was already talking about himself and my mother as we. And not only that but he was shoving his putrid daughter in my face; little miss perfect, teacher's pet, Imelda.

"Your mother says you can bring the dog," he said, indicating Bailey, who was digging around the well, "She'll also arrange for someone to collect your things. I may even look into hiring a van and doing it for you," he added.

"Not interested," I said, moving across and scooping Bailey into my arms.

"Well, will you just think about it, for your mother's sake?" He asked.

"No," I replied, simply.

"Lizzy, I think you should at least give this some thought. Your mother is very worried about you and would like you to be home with her. You know how she feels about animals; but, she is even prepared to allow a dog in her home, in order to make you happy."

"I am happy," I replied, "I'm always happy, when I am with my father, as was my mother, until you butted in and destroyed everything."

"My father did no such thing," Imelda snapped, "Your father did it all himself. I mean a man, who claims to love his wife, and then tries to force her to come back to a place she's scared of, is hardly a loving husband."

I calmly walked to the front door, slipping Bailey inside, before heading slowly back down the path and planting myself firmly in front of Imelda; my hand, shooting out and slapping her hard in the face.

"My father is an angel compared with yours and what he did, he did to save his family."

"You bitch!" Imelda screamed, recovered from the shock of the slap and flying into a rage. I had never heard little miss perfect swear before and was not prepared when her hand shot out and grabbed my hair.

Before I knew it, we were both rolling around on the ground; Mr Thomas, yelling at us to calm down, but neither of us was listening.

I heard footsteps, running across the yard and, as I clambered on top of Imelda, grabbing her by the ears and slamming her head into the dirt, I heard Jem yell out, "Go on Tiz, kick her ass!"

"Do you mind?" Mr Thomas snapped, bending down and trying to pull me of his darling daughter.

"Not at all," Jem replied, and I saw his arm shoot out, grabbing Mr Thomas by his shirt collar and spinning him towards his car.

Smiling, I climbed up off Imelda; who, at the sight of Jem manhandling her father, had broken into tears.

"Have my mum, Imelda," I said calmly, "Maybe she'll work out better for you than she did me," I hissed, then, wanting to add insult to injury, I added, "Let's hope she doesn't abandon you, like your own mother did."

I instantly regretted the last comment, as Imelda screamed in distress; her tears turning from a whine to hysterical wails.

"Your mother would be ashamed of you," Mr Thomas spat, as he rushed to Imelda's side and guided her into the car.

As he turned away from her to move around to the driver's side, she erased any guilt I had been feeling, as a smug smile, spread over her face and a finger shot up in my direction.

"That fucking bitch!" I snapped, flying for the car; but this time, Jem grabbed me.

"Let it go," he said, "People like that always get what they deserve, eventually."

CHAPTER 21

I was sat on the floor in the living room with Bailey in my lap and Beans, lounging beside me, while Jem sat on the sofa, leaning towards me; his hands wrapped around a steaming mug of coffee. My anger at the recent happenings had yet to recede and I was still burning with rage.

"I hate her!" I snapped, trying to vent some of that anger, "She thinks she's so god damned special. You should see her in school; always acting, as if butter wouldn't melt in her twisted, little mouth, when really, she's a manipulative, little bitch.

What makes it worse is how smart she is. I have to compete for the top spot with her in most of my lessons and that's fine; I don't mind competition. It makes it more interesting, but she has to go beyond that, has to play up to the teachers, offer to help them clean up after class; pin work up. She'd probably even wipe their asses, if she thought it would get her extra brownie points. Then there's the after school groups. She's in all of them, every single one, and running most of them; the committees, too, and now, now she's moving in on my mum. Just because her own mother ran out on her and her dad, when she was thirteen, doesn't mean she has a right to steal mine," I snapped.

I shifted slightly, turning to look at Jem, who was gazing into his coffee, as if deep in thought.

"I know my mum's a freak and sure, she probably fits with them better than dad and I; but, that's not the point, is it.

I mean, when I was younger, they were so happy; couldn't get enough of each other and then slowly that all changed and I just don't understand why," I hissed.

"People change, Tiz; that's just life," Jem said, looking across at me with sad eyes, "To be honest, I don't think it matters if parents stay together these days; you see it all the time, it's become the norm, and the way I see it, if they're happier apart, than they are together, then it's probably for the best."

"But, they're not happier apart. You've seen dad; he tries to act happy, but he's miserable. I just wish she wasn't such an idiot. I mean, dad's a hundred times better than Mr frigging Thomas and dad loves her; really loves her."

"Yeah, he probably does and, in some ways, she probably loves him, too; but sometimes that's not enough, not if people want different things. Maybe you should try talking to your mum; you know, get her side of the story, find out why she doesn't want to be with your dad anymore. There might be more to it than you realise, Tiz."

I gnawed at my bottom lip, as he spoke; frowning at his words. What made him think I had any interest in hearing mum's excuses? That was all I would get from her; excuse after excuse. and I could probably guess what most of them would be faster than she could say them.

Deciding to ignore Jem's suggestion, I gazed towards the window and carried on my rant, "I mean, what the hell was she thinking, sending them over here? She knows I can't stand Imelda. I mean, why the hell would someone do that?"

"Maybe she didn't. Maybe they came off their own backs."

"Oh, she sent them, alright," I snapped, " and what if dad had of been here, how would he feel seeing them; not to mention what it would have done to him, if he'd had to listen to Mr Thomas, going on about him and mum, as if they were already an item. You should have heard him; it was we this, and we that. Just thinking about it makes me want to scream. I really hate them Jem; I mean, properly hate them," I cried.

"Just forget about them; they're not worth the upset. You know what I think?" he asked, and I shook my head sadly, "I think you need to look at this in a different way. I mean, that Imelda girl; what's she really got, other than good grades and a father that looks like Humpty Dumpty, but you, you've got so much more, Tiz. I mean seriously, you've got me for a start," he said, putting his coffee cup down and jumping to his feet, arms outstretched, as he spun in a slow circle, "Think about it, Tiz. How many girls get to have their own on site stud to play with?" He said, arching his eyebrows; a mischievous grin, plastered in place. I had to laugh at his antics. That was the problem with Jem; he had a way of making you laugh, even when every part of you was ready to break down in despair.

Gently pushing Bailey off my lap and onto the floor, I leaned towards Jem; grabbing for his legs, which I then tugged out from under him, bursting into fits of laughter, as he flew backwards, crashing into the sofa with a thud.

"For a stud, you sure go down easy," I joked.

"Well, you know Tiz, not all men are afraid to..." he let the end of the sentence hang in the air, but we both knew exactly what he meant, "'Cause," he added, giving me a wry smile, "us men need a good cooked breakfast, some nice soft pillows to lay our weary head on at the end of the day, and of course, lots of kisses, if we're going to keep ourselves fit for service."

"Oh. Well, in that case, I think you're in the wrong house," I replied, lifting Bailey into my arms, as I jumped to my feet.

"We'll see," he called, as I scurried from the room, "Go get your jodhpurs on," he added, "We're going for a ride."

"What about Bailey?"

"Your dad should be home soon. I'm sure he'll watch him for you," Jem replied, getting to his feet, "I'll nip over to the farm and pick up my horse and be back here in about forty-five minutes, so you better be ready," he added.

I nodded, deciding a ride was just what I needed to take my mind off today's events, and headed for my room; Bailey, still safely wrapped in my arms.

*

When Jem pulled into the yard, almost an hour later, dad and I were sat on the wall, surrounding the front of the house, watching Bailey chasing an imaginary intruder.

Jem climbed out of the truck, waved, and moved around to the back of the horse trailer. I watched with interest, wondering what sort of horse Jem would own, and was not surprised, when he led out a large bay gelding that had to be at least eighteen hands. He was a stunning looking horse and seemed unfazed, as he was led out of the horsebox, already tacked up and ready to go.

"Is Misty ready?" Jem asked, referring to the little dapple grey mare he had brought over for me to ride.

I nodded and headed into the barn, where I had left her munching on some pony nuts, and led her out to the yard. Next to Jem's beautiful gelding, she looked less than impressive; but, I mounted her calmly, trying not to let my disappointment show.

My dad waved us off, as we headed out onto the moors; Beans, weaving around in front of us, determined, it seemed, to sniff every blade of grass.

"I thought we could ride over to Rough Tor, then

across to Davidstow, and perhaps follow the roads back, but you have to be careful on the lanes; some of the locals fly around the bends, without much thought."

"Sounds good; well, bar the risk of reckless drivers," I replied jokingly.

"Did you tell your dad about your little visitors earlier?" Jem enquired, turning the conversation serious, once more.

"I had to. It wouldn't have been right to let him get an ear bashing from my mum, without having had a chance to prepare."

"Your dad's pretty chilled; I shouldn't think he'd let it worry him, too much."

"I hope not," I replied, encouraging Misty into a trot.

Jem was soon beside me, matching my pace, a calm smile on his face.

"I like it at your place; nice to get some peace and quiet. Everything's always so manic at ours."

"Must be nice though; having a big family," I replied, thinking back to all the times I'd wished for a brother or sister to play with, when all my friends had gone home.

"If you like competing for attention, getting a whack for something ya didn't even do, and people nicking all your stuff, when you're not looking, then sure it's a hoot," he replied, sarcastically.

"Oh, come on; there must be upsides."

"Morwena's alright, I guess, but she's crafty; she only has to flutter her eyelids to get gramps, jumping to attention."

"I guess it's because she's a girl and I hear being the youngest can help, when your part of a big family."

"I guess," Jem replied, but he didn't seem at all convinced, "I've got this aunt; she's my dad's sister and her and gramps had some kind of falling out, when she wasn't much older than you and Morwena. We don't see her and I have certainly never met her, but I've often wondered if my gramps thinks he was too harsh on her or something, and that maybe that's why he's so soft on Morwena, now."

"Do you know what they fell out over?" I asked, wondering just how open Jem's family was with him.

"Something to do with her having an abortion, I believe. Gramps was furious and never forgave her; but, I can kind of see it from her point of view. I mean, she was young and unmarried. People were funny about that back then, weren't they? It must have been pretty scary for her."

"Probably; but, at the end of the day, it was her body and her choice. Your grandfather needs to accept that."

Jem simply nodded at this, then pointed up at the sky, "See the buzzard?" He asked.

I gazed into the sky, watching the bird floating on the breeze, scanning the moors below for prey, and wondered if it was the same bird that I had seen before. The moors looked beautiful; made up of a mishmash of different greens, some patches, pale and faded, as if it were a carpet in a newly emptied room, the worn spots, glaringly obvious, against the bright new patches that had, until recently, been protected by furniture.

Rough Tor was nearly upon us and the sounds of groups of walkers, chatting, carried to me, on the breeze.

"Must be nice to be a bird," I said, lost in thought, "Flying over everyone and everything; part of it, but distant from it."

Jem laughed at this, "Wow, very deep," he replied.

"Don't you ever wish you could escape all of the chaos in life and just float up into the sky, where it's peaceful?"

"Isn't that death?" He joked.

"Oh, very funny," I hissed.

"Way I see it; you've just got to take every day as it comes. If it's a bad day, you look forward to the end, and if it's a good day you savour it; but, whatever happens, you should just be thankful you survived it and that tomorrow's another day. Sitting there, wishing you could float up in the sky and away from it all is just dreaming of the impossible, and to be fair, Tiz, you ain't got it all that bad, right now. You've got a nice home, where admittedly, there are some issues, but they'll fix themselves, in time, and you've got an awesome dad, not to mention a nice, new pup. You're sixteen, so you're nearing the completion of your school life and preparing for college or Uni, whatever's your thing, and after that, hopefully, a good career. You, my dear, have your whole life ahead of you; so, why sweat it. As for your mum, just remember how you felt about what she did and don't make the same mistakes with your kids," I listened to his speech with interest. He was smarter than he looked and constantly surprised me, "Race you to Rough Tor," I said, with a smile, and pushed Misty forward.

We charged across the moors at speed; Beans, sprinting along beside us, his legs pumping beneath him, coat, gleaming in the sun. He was a truly beautiful dog and incredibly fast. Jem held his horse back, letting me win. Reaching Rough Tor, we slowed the horses to a walk, both of us laughing and beaming with joy.

"We'll have to do this more often," I said, as we crossed a low bridge over a stream, stopping on the other side to allow Beans and the horses to drink, before we headed up towards Rough Tor car park.

When we were half-way up the hill to the car park, both of us dismounted the horses and turned around to look out over the moors. There we stood, side by side, gazing up at the rocky top of Rough Tor. I rubbed affectionately at Misty's neck. She was a nice horse, carried herself well, had a good stride, and could apparently get up a good speed, despite her size.

"Nice, ain't she?" Jem said, as if reading my thoughts, "It was your dad, who picked her out for you," he said.

"Huh?"

"She's not ours, Tiz," he replied, with a smile, "Your dad had her picked out, long before you moved into Reno;

was out riding her, all the time, to make sure she was sound, before he'd buy her. He did the same with three others, too; but, they didn't make the cut. He said you'd want a big horse and, believe me, he tried out a couple that were huge; but, she was the nicest out of the lot and a real good horse, not to mention bombproof."

"So, why didn't you tell me before?" I asked.

"Because your dad said she'd need to grow on you; but I'd say, by the way you were just gazing at her that she already has."

I looked at Misty again, this time highly perplexed, and realised grudgingly that my father was right; I would have chosen a bigger horse for myself. In fact, I probably would have walked right past Misty without giving her so much as a glance.

"Sucks, when your parents have you sussed, don't it?" Jem said; a wicked grin on his face.

"So, you were winding me up, when you said you wanted to observe my riding ability, before letting me on a better horse?"

"Pretty much; although, I noticed your position was a little sloppy on the trot," I merely glared at him, before leading Misty up onto the grassy slope, so she could graze for a while.

Jem soon joined me on the grass, giving his horse's neck a gentle rub, before leaving him to graze quietly. He then moved across to a smooth patch of ground, where he sat and looked out across the moors.

I stood there beside him; both of us watching a couple as they slowly made their way down from Rough Tor, arm in arm. After a while, I sat down next him; smiling, as I watched him rub vigorously at Beans' belly.

"We're pretty lucky really, if you think about it," he said, "I mean, all the people that come here for day trips, when the weather's nice, have to head back to the towns and cities, after, but us, we get to live here and enjoy this every day of our lives."

"Now, who's being deep?" I said, digging him in the ribs.

His mouth creased into a smile at my words, then he flung an arm around my neck and pulled me close.

"You're some piece of work," he said, with a smile, then leaned down, his eyes locked on mine, as our lips met, making me beam inside; not wanting this kiss to end. Feeling his arms encircle my waist, I slipped my own around his strong neck; a shiver of excitement, washing over me, as his fingertips found the bare skin of my back and began to stroke. If there really was a heaven on earth, this had to be it.

CHAPTER 22

The next day, all was chaos at the house; as my father rushed to get everything ready for the grand opening of the surgery, planned for that afternoon.

Dad and Jem had decided to keep the actual date from me, in the end, so that I would not be distracted from my studies; trying to help with the preparations. I honestly wasn't all that bothered; as the thought of sticking up flyers and hanging up banners was a less than pleasing one to me.

In the morning dad introduced Jem and me to the people he had hired to work alongside him.

There was a local girl in her mid-twenties called Shelly, who Jem seemed to know very well. She would be the full time receptionist for the clinic. I took to Shelly instantly, due to her bubbly personality, which seemed to be as large as her frame; not counting her cleavage, which was strangely lacking. Everything about Shelly screamed fun; even her hair, which was a frizzy mass of blonde that puffed out around her face in an almost clownish fashion, but despite this, her dimpled cheeks gave her an almost cute and cuddly appearance that made you feel instantly at ease. On seeing Bailey, she immediately collapsed to the floor, cooing affectionately at him; everyone else in the room, quickly forgotten.

Next, there was a tall, thin lady, already caped in a long white vet's coat; her black hair, pulled up in a tight bun that sat on her head, at a slight angle, and sprouted tufts of hair, here and there. Clearly, she was not as fussy as my mother was.

Standing next to her, I was reminded of a stick insect, as there was barely an inch of flesh on her, and her nose was long and tapered at the tip. Her eyes were small and dark and when she laughed, it was loud and somewhat painful to the ears. Yet, she seemed nice; if a little bit posh, and was extremely excited to be a part of the team. Her name was Alison.

Next, were two girls who had worked with my father in Bude; abandoning their jobs there as veterinary nurses the instant they found out my father was starting his own practice.

They were both in their late forties, had brown hair, were of medium build, and around five foot three in height. They were old friends of the family, however, as similar as they were in looks; they were very different, when it came to personalities; Hannah, being very stern and bossy, while Mary was quiet and motherly.

Lastly, there was a fairly young vet; only twenty-three, who had just completed his veterinary training. He stood shyly to one side, nervously gnawing at his fingernails. He was of average height with a pleasant face and had a slight stutter, when he talked; but, like the rest, he seemed pleasant, and excited, if somewhat nervous, at the prospect of his first official day as a fully qualified vet.

Another receptionist had also been hired; but, she had been unable to make it for the grand opening, due to her second job. My father explained that her name was Cathy and that she would be working the weekend shifts. He also assured us that she was a lovely lady, who he was certain we would find pleasant and easy to get along with.

That morning, between talking and getting to know

each other, we all ran around, preparing for what we hoped, would be a large gathering of potential new clients.

At ten to twelve the first car arrived. Jem's mum, bursting out of it with the biggest cheesecake I had ever seen.

"You've got to have food," she called, as she rushed towards dad; pausing midway, as she realised she couldn't hug him, without squashing the gigantic cake. Looking for the nearest victim, which turned out to be Hannah, she thrust the cake towards her and with a smile, cooed, "Be a doll and dump that in the kitchen, dear," before hurrying back to dad, whose head she swiftly shoved, between her jiggling bosoms; an experience, I'm sure, my father found, far more enjoyable than Jem or I had.

"Why are you all just standing there?" she snapped, releasing dad and flinging an arm in the direction of the car, "There's plenty more, where that beauty came from, so you best get a move on."

We all hurried into action, rushing to the car, where we were met by hundreds of carefully wrapped food parcels.

"…and the back" She called, smiling happily, as Mary scurried around, to the rear of the Land Rover.

"Oh my," Mary cried, a few seconds later, "I'm not touching that," she hissed, stepping away hurriedly.

"It's just a pig for roasting," Jenny cried, "My god, some people," she added, rushing over to the back of the four by four and tugging on a large, green mat, "Here, come and give me a hand with this, Jem," she called, waving the rest of us, out of the way.

"You can all wipe those looks of disgust off your faces, right now! They'll be smelling this cooking from miles away and that'll have the beggars running," she chirped, "There ain't no man round abouts that don't love a nice bit of pork; you, mark my words. And, I dare say, you'll all be keen enough to sink your teeth into it, too; once my boy's done with the roasting," she added.

I wasn't a vegetarian, not by any means; but, I had to admit that, even I, was startled at the sight of the dead pig that Jem helped lift from the back of the Land Rover. It was one thing to eat pork; but, to see a whole pig, head and all, heading for the spit roast, was something I wasn't quite prepared for.

"You really shouldn't have gone to so much trouble, Jenny," my father said, beaming from ear to ear, at the sight of the large, unmoving animal; as if all his Christmases had just come at once.

"Trouble? It's no trouble John," she called, "I've sent Morwena and Tristan off round the local villages, making sure everyone comes, and they're going to get some banners up on the way here, too. Gotta make sure they all know, where you are, haven't we? It's a good thing I had a nosy round for your advertising if you can call it that. All I found was a pitiful advert in the local rag. I doubt anyone would have spotted it. Mark my words John; if you wanna get people's attention, you gotta kick up an almighty stink and the tastier the stink, the better," she sung; stabbing a finger at the pig.

I watched as Jem hefted the dead animal, up onto his shoulder, before carrying it off, across the yard. When he reached the picnic table, he simply swept an arm over the surface then dumped the lifeless pig on top.

He, too, was sporting a large grin as he headed towards the barn and I couldn't help but laugh. What was it with men and dead animals that seemed to automatically put them in a good mood?

*

It took some work to get all of the food that Jenny had prepared, laid out, and by the time we were finished, every surface in the kitchen was covered with plates and bowls that were full to bursting with tasty treats.

Dad wandered around the kitchen nervously; less than pleased that the general public would have to be allowed access to the house, in order to stock their plates.

"We're going to have to make sure they don't go into any of the other rooms," he said, as the staff gathered round, "what with the history of this place and all the stories that have been flying around for years about the murders and such. There's bound to be people that are a bit curious, so can we please try and make sure that there is someone in here at all times with the guests, keeping them from wandering off around the rest of the house?"

The staff all agreed to this wholeheartedly, but dad seemed not to be done with them, yet. Knowing better than to stick around and listen to him harping on, I headed out into the yard; leaving my father and his new employees to it.

I found Jem, over near the barn; clearly in his element, as he basted the large pig, now firmly fixed on a long spit, over what looked like, half of an old oil drum, filled with coal.

"Where did you get that from?" I asked, indicating his new toy, and knowing full well that it hadn't been brought over with all the food.

"Barn," he said, as he examined his now, well basted pig.

"What is it with men and dead animals?" I asked, trying to pull his attention away from his new toy.

"It's not just a dead animal," he replied, calmly, "It's a rite of passage. There are just some things that a man has to do to truly feel like a man."

"Oh," I said, smiling wickedly, "you mean like hunting, providing, and I don't know, protecting?" I added, with a shrug.

"Exactly," he replied, with the biggest, most contented smile I'd ever seen.

"So, you killed it?" I asked.

"No. We're not allowed to anymore; not if it's for public consumption, at any rate," he replied, so seriously that it was a struggle not to laugh.

"Well, you didn't provide it," I added, quickly, "because it was your mum, who did that, wasn't it?"

"Technically," he replied, gazing at me suspiciously now.

"So, then this would be what, exactly?" I asked then added, "Because, if you didn't hunt it and you didn't provide it, then you must be..," I let the end of the sentence hang in the air and then studied his face, just waiting for the penny to drop, "Pro..," I offered slowly, when it didn't seem, as if he was ever going to get it, on his own.

"Oh," he said, a smile spreading over his face; not the reaction I had been expecting at all, "You think I'm protecting it," he added, the mischievous grin, now plastered on his face, while I gazed at him, perplexed.

"Well, I'm protecting something," he continued, with a smirk, "but, it ain't the pig,"

Realising what he was talking about, I simply glared at him then turned on my heels; deciding it was best to let this one slide. After all, there was no way I was going to spend the rest of the day, roasting a dead pig, just to prove him wrong.

"See, women these days aren't as tough as they used to be," he called out, across the yard, not content to just let it go, "Once upon a time, a woman could take an animal, just like this one, and cook it all up by herself, but nowadays, women tend to be more squeamish; which means, us men have to go and protect them from the reality of good old fashioned fresh meat. I mean seriously, Tiz; there are women today that don't even know how to poach an egg. Can you believe that?"

I didn't have to look back to know that he was smirking. Realising that there was really only one response that was fitting of a situation such as this, I simply shook my head and gave him the finger.

*

By 2pm, the yard and kitchen were at the bursting point and I was feeling somewhat overwhelmed, as Shelly and Morwena dragged me around the mass of people; introducing me to so many new faces that I had no hope of ever remembering any of their names.

Dad, too, was receiving the same treatment at the hands of Jenny, and every so often, he would smile across at me; clearly enjoying the process a lot more than I was.

Jem had remained by his hog the whole time, supervising its cooking with care and chasing away the local kids, who kept begging for some crackling.

It seemed as if everyone within a ten mile radius had shown up at the farm for the grand opening of dad's new veterinary practice, although, as of yet, I had not seen anyone be led through into the actual practice itself; so, when I spotted dad, ushering a group of people in through the main doors to the practice, I breathed a sigh of relief.

As happy as I was to see that all was going well for dad and his new endeavour, I was missing the peace and tranquillity that had become the norm at Reno; not to mention Bailey, who I'd had to leave locked up in his crate in my bedroom, due to the large number of people, who had naturally brought their dogs along with them.

Deciding to use Bailey as an excuse for a bit of peace and quiet, I headed back into the house; slipping past a rather harassed looking Mary, who it seemed had been left to shoo away the curious on her own.

As I reached the hall, I heard Bailey whining, above, and hurried up the stairs. Although, Beans had been left with him for company, it seemed he wasn't best pleased about being locked away, when there was so much excitement going on, below. Pushing the bedroom door open, I carefully slipped inside, letting the door shut, behind me.

"Hi, boy's," I said, giving Bean's head a quick rub, before rushing to make a fuss of Bailey, whose crate was now awash with teddy bear stuffing.

"You keep destroying all your toys like this and I won't be buying you any more, mister," I hissed, jabbing a finger at my fat little pup playfully, before getting back up and heading across the room to my desk, where I'd left his squeaky toy, earlier.

Pausing at the desk briefly, I looked out over the yard; smiling, as I watched Jem dishing up his beloved pig, my father chatting happily with Alison, a huge smile plastered on his face, and Morwena, flirting outrageously with a tall, rugged looking lad that she had introduced to me earlier as Martin.

I thought back over the last few weeks here at Reno and realised that, for the most part, I was very happy to be able to call this my home. Of course, there had been a few problems, but watching all the people, below, milling around happily; the unease that I had felt, of late, seemed to have diminished.

Moving across to my bed, I threw open the window and sat, listening to the chatter below. We'd never done anything like this at the cottage. When we'd had parties there, it had been more of a formal dinner, at which people chatted politely about boring topics. This however, was not like that at all; people laughed and joked, kids ran around playing, and everyone was simply enjoying the beautiful day and friendly company. Everyone, I realised, except Tristan; who I spotted leaning up against the side of his mum's Land Rover, staring off into space, as if deep in thought.

Climbing off the bed, I extracted Bailey from his crate and hurried down the stairs; Beans, close on my heels, as we slipped quietly, out of the front door.

Beans, spotting the fun outside of the garden was quickly off, over the wall; leaving poor Bailey to play on his own in the front yard. Still, I didn't have time to worry about that now, and placing Bailey down, I moved over to the side of the garden and started to wave in Tristan's direction; desperately trying to get his attention. I was relieved, when he spotted me and slowly made his way through the crowd towards me.

"Bit much for you?" I asked, as he reached me.

"Yeah, I'm not really one for small talk," he replied, turning round and gazing out, across the yard.

"I guessed as much; so I thought I'd save you. Dad's got the house under guard, which means it's lovely and peaceful inside, except for the kitchen. If you want, you can come up in my room for a while. I'll even sit down and shut up, if you're all talked out."

"That," he said, with a smile, "sounds perfect; well, all but the part where you shut up," he added, with a grin.

I smiled at his words, and picking up Bailey, led Tristan up the stairs to my room.

As we talked, I wondered what it was about Tristan that Jem hated so much; after all, Tristan seemed smart and pretty laid back. It was clear, however, that, other than having the same parents, they had nothing in common. Tristan for a start was able to hold a whole conversation without once flirting or making fun of me; but, like Jem, I found Tristan very easy to get along with and was surprised to find that he was also very artistic, although his sketches were somewhat darker than my own.

As I flicked through the small sketch book that he carried around with him in his back pocket, I was met with images of mythical beasts, demons, and vampires with lips curled back and dripping fangs. And, although not really to my taste, there was no denying that he had talent.

"The eyes are amazing," I said, indicating a picture of a

young girl, bound to a stake, as a large demon, clawed at her flesh, "You capture the fear in them, perfectly," I added.

"I try," he replied, smiling.

"And you just imagine this all up and draw it from the images in your head?" I asked, amazed.

"Pretty much, although sometimes I draw stuff from films, I've seen, or comics I've read,"

I nodded and continued to flick through the book, wondering what it was that attracted him to such dark art.

"I'd love to create my own comics one day, but my writing needs a bit of work," he said, looking out of the window, across the moors, "that or write a fantasy novel; but, I think a comic would be a more realistic goal."

"You should do a writing course or something," I said smiling, "You can do them at home now or over the internet."

"I will, eventually; but, I've got to save up for it first and well, I don't get much for helping out round the farm. That's the problem with working for family; you kinda have to be grateful that they give you anything at all. The only problem is I think my parents still see it as just me working for my pocket money, but I've been looking around for a part time job; just something simple, so I can earn a few extra quid."

I nodded; once again, realising just how lucky I was. I'd never had to work for my money; had never even had a set allowance. If I wanted something, I simply had to ask for it and my father would hand over the cash.

I looked at the clock as I heard footsteps on the stairs and realised that Tristan and I had been hiding away up here for over an hour.

"That'll probably be dad, wondering where I've got to," I said, as there was a rap on my bedroom door, but when it was pushed open, it was not my father standing there, but Jem, who quickly took in the scene; the smile, vanishing from his face, as he spotted Tristan sitting beside me on the window seat.

His eyes narrowing, he glared at Tristan and then moved across the room, pulling me roughly, out of my seat and into his arms; his eyes, never leaving his brother's, as he embraced me. Then spinning me round, his arm, locked around my shoulders, as if any minute this hug might turn into a noogie. He stood there, unspeaking, the two brothers, seemingly locked in a silent conversation, as they both stared at each other; Tristan slowly shaking his head, while Jem nodded his.

"I'm sorry, did I miss something?" I asked.

"I didn't realise you were dating now," Tristan said; the tension, clear in his voice.

"Well, you know how it is bro, you meet a beautiful woman; it's only natural that we'd get attracted to each other and decide to start a life together."

"What?" I said, looking up at Jem, perplexed. We had only kissed once; well, bar the peck, when he had slept outside my bedroom door that night. Sure, there had been plenty of flirting; but, here he was making it sound as if we were about to get married, when I hadn't even been sure that we were officially dating.

"Looks like that's news to Tiz," Tristan replied, smirking at Jem.

"Well, that's because I haven't asked her to marry me yet," Jem said, as calmly as if he was announcing that he needed the loo.

"Oh, this should be good," Tristan snipped, while I prayed that Jem was not about to do what I thought he was.

"If you think I'm going to do it now, right here in front of you, think again. I want that to be special," Jem snarled, stabbing a finger towards his brother, as I let out a sigh of relief.

"I'm only telling you, because I want to make it clear

that you are wasting your time. I know your game Bro and you can jog on, Tiz is mine; and even if she wasn't, I wouldn't let you within a mile of her."

It was safe to say I was getting a little irritated now. How dare he say I was his; like I was some possession? Whatever the rivalry between these brothers, I did not want to get caught in the middle of it.

"Wow, you just want everything don't you, Jem?" Tristan snapped, "One farm, isn't good enough for you, you have to go and sink your claws into another. And, what happens when you get your hands on this one, huh?"

"You fucking twisted little prick," Jem snarled, removing his arm from my shoulder and getting up in his brother's face.

"Let me make something perfectly clear to you, Tristan. Unlike you, I am not a money-grabbing little shit, and if this beautiful woman here actually makes me the happiest man on the planet and her father were to leave her this farm, then this will be the only one we'll have. Our family farm will go to someone worthwhile, who deserves a break, and that, asshole, is not you."

"And you think Granddad would let you give the place away just like that?" Tristan snarled back.

"Oh, I think Granddad would be more than happy with my choice; after all, I would be giving it to his favourite granddaughter."

"Morwena?" Tristan gasped, "You can't be serious. She'd run it into the ground."

"She'll marry someone, eventually, and if it's Martin out there, then she'll do just fine. Even if she doesn't marry Martin, or someone like him, she'll still do a damn sight better job of it than you."

"You're determined to wipe me out of this family aren't you, Jem? You'd sooner see me on the street, than give me even an ounce of what I'm owed."

"Owed? No one owes you anything. You're a lazy,

arrogant, piece of shit, and the worst thing that ever happened to this family was you. We'd all be better off, if you just went all depressant and topped yourself."

"Jem!" I cried, unable to believe he could be so cruel.

"Tiz, you have no idea what he's like. He comes in here and puts on an act for you; but, the reality is a less than pleasant one. You have to believe me."

"Whatever he has done, you don't just turn around and tell someone you wish they would top themselves; it's out of order," I hissed.

"Tiz, listen to me," he said, taking my face in his hands and gazing down into my eyes, "Tristan is a liar. He will tell you anything in order to get what he wants. You saw how quickly he assumed the only reason I wanted you was because I wanted your farm. That's because that's what he wants."

I looked at Tristan then, wondering if what Jem was saying was true, but Tristan was simply shaking his head; a look of disgust, on his face.

"Look, I don't know what you two have against each other; but, you can leave me out of it, okay?" I hissed, then turned and hurried from the room.

*

"Are you mad at me?" Jem said, coming into the living room, later that night, where I was sat, doing some revision.

I had managed to avoid him, all day, as I mingled with the guests and I wasn't sure I was ready to deal with him, just yet. My head was awash with questions though. Had he really meant what he had said, or simply said it to chase Tristan away?

"What do you think?" I snapped, "I wasn't even sure we were actually dating and then you go and claim that we are about to walk down the aisle, and not only that, but you talk about me as if I'm a thing instead of a human being. I am not yours Jem, I am owned by no one and never will be."

"I know. I'm sorry, it just came out. You just don't understand what Tristan is like, and I didn't lie; not really. Tiz, I really care about you. You drive me wild. I've never felt that way about anyone, before, and I'm not being big headed here, but normally it's me driving the women crazy; but you, you're just so tough. Sometimes I'm certain you are as into me as I am you and then other times, I feel as if you could take me or leave me.

If I was ready to get married, I know it would be you that I would want as my wife, and although, at present, I'm not, I know that I love you."

I was so shocked at his words. Was he really being serious, for once? He looked serious, but it was hard to tell with Jem; he was smooth, smart, and I wasn't altogether sure that he wouldn't lie, simply to get himself out of a hole.

"Look," I said, "I have no interest in your brother, beyond friendship, and I'm not sure what we are or what we might be one day; but, I can tell you now, if you drag me into the middle of this feud you have with your brother again, we're never going to be anything. I have enough problems of my own, right now, and I just want life to be as drama free as possible."

"I know you hate him; I get that, but I'm a big girl Jem, I can take care of myself, and if you're so certain he is just trying to get his hands on this farm, then I'm sure, when he realises I have no interest in him, other than as a friend, he'll soon get bored and clear off anyway."

Jem nodded at this and then held out his arms to me. I moved into them, grateful for the warmth; but, when he leaned down to kiss me, I pulled away.

"Don't push your luck Jem Trerise," I said; not willing to forgive him fully, just yet.

CHAPTER 23

A week had passed, since the grand opening of the surgery, and dad had a steady stream of clients at the clinic, as well as a new spring in his step.

I, meanwhile, was preparing to return to school and had been throwing myself into my course work. I was actually quite looking forward to getting back to my old routine and seeing Calvin, my best friend; who, despite having attempted to call him several times over half term, I had not spoken to, since a week before school had ended for the holidays.

I realised that he had no idea about where I was currently living or everything that had happened, since the move, and knew that he would be desperate for all the gossip, once he found out; assuming, of course, he was still alive or had even returned to the UK, after his Spanish holiday, which, bearing in mind how determined he had been to meet a hunky Spanish guy and stay in the Costa del Sol, might not be too far from the truth.

It didn't take long for reality to kick in, however, as I remembered that this was Calvin I was thinking about and that even I, his best friend, could only cope with him in small doses. I decided that, in all likelihood, he had simply forgotten to take his phone charger with him and had, in fact, been stapled to a chair by his parents and forced to study.

Having neglected my revision somewhat over the holidays myself, I'd begun to feel as if I, too, was stapled to my chair; although, admittedly it was guilt that was forcing me in place and not my parents. I was determined to cram as much revision in as possible; therefore, when Jem greeted me in the kitchen early Monday morning, after having spent a long night, buried in my books, I was a little bit distracted.

"Looking forward to your first day, back at school?" He asked, as he made scrambled eggs and I gave Bailey his breakfast.

I simply grunted; my enthusiasm about returning to school largely diminished, after a long night of joy sapping revision, which had done little in the way of helping me feel prepared for my upcoming exams.

"What classes you got today?" Jem asked.

"R.E., Maths, English, Art, and Spanish," I replied, with a groan, really not looking forward to any of them.

"You're doing Religious Education?" He asked, puzzled.

"Yes, I'm good at it, which means I have a good chance of getting an A and if I want to make it into a good veterinary school, I need all the A's I can get."

"Fair enough," he replied, with a smile, as he began to dish up, "Your dad said you liked school."

"I do. I'm just behind that's all. I should have got a lot more revision done than I have."

"So, who's gonna know?" He replied, sliding a plate across the table, where I was now stood, stuffing my books into my bag.

"I'll know," I said, then cursed, as I realised I'd left my writing pad, upstairs.

"What's the matter?" Jem asked, as I turned and left the room, "Your breakfast is going to get cold," he called after me, but I ignored him.

I hurried through to the living room and round into what had become dad's study, figuring I would grab one of his A4 pads and save myself a trip upstairs. I rifled through the mass of paperwork stacked on top of his pile of pads and yanked one free, knocking a few sheets of paper, which had been tucked underneath, to the floor, in the process.

I bent down to retrieve them, my eyes falling on the word 'deadly' and I paused, gazing down at the letter intently. I had never read my father's correspondence before, but my interest was piqued and so, listening to see if there was any noise from above, where I assumed my father was still sleeping, I began to read...

Dear Mr Bray,

An article I read recently in the local paper about your clinic caught my attention and raised some concerns for me.

As a young girl, I lived close to the property, the outbuildings of which you have turned into a surgery, and I know a great deal about its history, and thus know that you living there, especially with a young daughter, poses some risks.

I know you must think me raving mad and will no doubt think me even more so, when I express some of my fears to you; however, I beg that you at least contact me, so that I can explain in greater detail.

Here, I will simply say that your choosing to remain in the house could be a very deadly choice, indeed.

There are people who long to have possession of that particular property and whom I fear will stop at nothing to get the deed in their hands.

Please contact me on the number listed above ASAP. I know you may think me crazy, but I am merely trying to protect you and your family.

~Emily

I gazed down at the piece of paper, perplexed; wondering if my father had contacted this woman or not, although, knowing my father, it was highly unlikely.

I hurriedly snatched up a pen and scribbled the number, as well as her name, onto my new pad and then replaced the letter under the next pad in the pile.

"Come on Tiz. You're never going to have time to eat, if you don't get a move on," I heard Jem call from the kitchen, as I hurriedly ripped the page off the pad, folded it, and stuffed it into my pocket.

CHAPTER 24

When Jem pulled up at the school gates, I spotted Calvin, slouched against the mesh of the fence that surrounded the school's playground; a fag, hanging from the corner of his mouth.

I waved to him and jumped from the truck, barrelling into his arms and squeezing him tight.

"You're not going to believe where I'm living," I cried, pulling back from him and gazing up into his face.

"Spain was dull, not that you asked," he hissed, feigning indignation.

"Why dull?" I asked, linking my arm through his and coaxing him slowly towards the truck.

"My parents dragged me around everywhere with them, adamant that I play the part of translator, then locked me in my room at night with a heap of books and insisted I study, while they went out to fine restaurants and ate themselves fat. To make things worse, I dropped my mobile in the pool the first day and they then used my need for a new one as a bartering tool to get me to study; a phone, I might add, that has yet to be given to me."

"Well you did need to do some revision while you were there, Cal, I mean, we have got some really important exams coming up."

"I am fully aware of the impending, dream crushing,

degrading farce that is pressing down on us, as we speak, with no regard for those who are allergic to written tests."

"You're not allergic," I said, stopping and looking up at him, "you just get nervous, and the more you revise, the easier it will be to get past that."

"That's easy for you to say, miss straight A's, but you have never experienced the suffocation that results from my and, I might add, many others allergies to tests and yes I do say allergies, for only allergies can cause such reaction as inability to breath, itching, and sweats. Still, they insist on ignoring this fact and forcing us all to partake with little regard for our state of health; all so they can classify us into groups, based on our ability to perform in a task that, frankly, is unfair and unrealistic."

"And breathe," I joked.

"I'm serious, my life will be ruined, my full potential never realised, and all because they insist on having written exams."

"I'll get you some Claritin," I chirped, ignoring his scowl, and dragged him over to the truck, where Jem stood glaring at Calvin with annoyance.

"Oh, yum!" Calvin cried, his distress suddenly forgotten at the sight of Jem, "Oh something that good looking just has to be gay. Tell me he's gay," he pleaded, then went into a mini-sulk, when I shook my head.

Jem's frown instantly turned into a smile, as he pulled me from Calvin and draped a somewhat possessive arm around my shoulder. I was less than impressed; but, noticing Imelda watching, from up near the playing fields, I let it go and smiled at Calvin, who was brushing a hand through his mop of brown hair. His blue eyes locked on Jem's fingers, which were running gently through my own hair.

"Jem, this is Calvin," I said, as way of introduction.

"Hi," Jem responded.

"Jem," Calvin replied with raised eyes, "Jem, indeed; a

good looking straight man. Oh, how the ladies must love you or are you bi-sexual?" He asked; hope, glinting in his eyes.

"Straight," Jem replied quickly, and Calvin instantly released his, somewhat flabby, tummy and sighed sulkily.

"So, are you an item?" He asked, waving his arm erratically between the two of us.

"No," I cried, quickly.

"Yes," Jem chirped, at the same time, while Calvin simply raised an eyebrow.

"Maybe." Both Jem and I replied, in unison.

"No, yes, maybe; well, that's a very helpful answer," Calvin hissed, rolling his eyes, "So, where did you meet, how long's it been going on, and why the fuck did you not call me?" He growled.

"I tried," I replied, ignoring the rest of his questions.

"Oh yeah; phone, pool, I forgot, but never mind that now, tell me all about the new house. Is it big, small, pretty, shitty, modern, or old?"

"It's big," I said, then paused to think, "It's very old," I added, "and several people were murdered there," I said, ignoring his gasp and adding, "by Insane frigging Reno."

"No!" Calvin exclaimed.

"Oh, yes," I said, and smiled knowingly.

"Oh my god!" He cried, "You cannot be serious."

"She is," Jem interjected.

"Oh, this is unreal. What's it like? Are there still blood stains? I mean, they never touched it; just shut it up, after the last ones didn't they, so there must be blood stains."

"Dad had it cleaned up, before we moved in, so it looks like any other old farm; but, we need to have it exorcised," I said, then frowned, as the bell rang.

"Tell me all about it, on the way to class." Calvin said, as I grabbed my bag from the truck.

"Nice meeting you, Jem," he chirped, with raised eyebrows, then turned to me and added, "I'll wait for you over there."

"Bye," Jem said, and shook his head, "Well, he's a character. Question is, would he be the maid of honour or...?"

"Neither, he's anti-weddings," I replied, hurriedly cutting him off, "I have to go, or I'll be late," I said, and then stood there dumbly, unsure what to do.

Jem, however, was not so uncertain and he lent forward and whispered in my ear, "Imelda's still watching."

I hurriedly threw myself into his arms, locking my lips to his, and practically sucked his face off, in the process; only to turn round, after, and find that Imelda was nowhere in sight.

"Gotcha," Jem said, chuckling to himself. I merely glowered at him, then turned and ran after Calvin, who clearly had gotten bored waiting and was already half-way, across the playground.

CHAPTER 25

At lunchtime, Calvin and I walked to his house; both of us having passes that allowed us to leave school for our breaks.

Calvin was still trying to process everything I had told him about my time in my new home and was chatting away endlessly to himself, but all I could think about was the letter I had found. Who was this Emily, and what had she meant, when she said she was afraid that the people who wanted the house would stop at nothing to get it?

The only person that I was aware of who had a connection to the house, which was so strong that he had killed for it, was Reno and he was safely locked up, wasn't he; or was he? Maybe she knew something my father didn't, or perhaps he did and, like everything else, had simply withheld the information for fear of scaring me; but, would a man, who had murdered three families, have been released from prison, so soon.

Perhaps it was something to do with Jem's grandfather. Maybe that would explain mum's reaction to him; but then, from what I had seen of him, he hardly seemed the sort of person who would kill people and the Trerise family had done nothing but help us.

If it hadn't been for Jem's mum, the opening day would not have been such a success. Why would a family go out of their way to help us, if they wanted the house for themselves?

"I have to see it," Calvin cried suddenly, making me jump.

"See what?" I asked.

"The house, your new pup, everything," he cried, pulling me round to face him, "This weekend, roll out the red carpet, because Calvin is coming to stay."

"I'll ask," I replied.

"Oh, come on. Your dad's cool; he'll let me stay the night."

I knew he was probably right, but still, I wanted to ask, first. Dad had been so busy, lately, I was not sure he would be keen to deal with Calvin, who could be a headache at the best of times.

"I'll ask," I said, this time, more firmly, as he opened the gate and we hurried towards his front door.

"Do you think your mum would mind if I borrowed your phone?" I asked; the battery on mine having died in the car on the way to school this morning.

"Nah, she adores you, remember?" He said, with a smile.

As we entered into the front hall, his mum fell upon us, with sheer joy in her eyes.

"Tizzy, how are you darling? How's the new house? Do you like it? How are your parents? Have you all settled in yet or are you still trying to get things arranged? There's nothing worse than moving. They say it's one of the most stressful things you can do," she sang; her head, bobbing up and down like a nodding dog on a bumpy road.

"It's great," I said, neglecting to mention that mum was no longer living there with us, not that she actually had, after all, her few minutes stood in the kitchen could hardly be counted as living there.

"Oh, wonderful. Why don't you two go and get comfy and I'll bring you drinks and something nice to eat," she said, with a smile and hurried away, once more.

I loved Calvin's parents; especially his mum. She had long, brown hair that she rarely brushed and wore huge, woollen cardigans and baggy trousers, splattered, at all times, with paint, due to her artistic nature. Despite being short and dumpy, she was always full of energy and loved to have guests over; whether they had been invited or not, unlike my own mother. Even salesmen would be bustled through the door, as if they were old friends; only to find themselves quickly being outsold and leaving, sometimes hours later, with one or two of her paintings tucked under their arms, while having failed to sell anything, themselves.

His father in comparison was a giant, tall and thin, like a rake, with large, blue eyes and thick rimmed glasses. They looked very odd together; but, despite their differences, fit together perfectly when it came to their personalities.

"Mum, can Tiz use the phone?" Calvin called.

"Course," came the happy reply.

"I've just gotta nip to the loo, so knock yourself out," he said, with a smile, and rushed up the stairs.

I dropped down onto the bottom step and waited till I heard the bathroom door click shut, before picking up the receiver and hurriedly dialling the number.

"Hello?" A female voice said, after only a couple of rings.

"Hi, can I speak to Emily?" I asked.

"Speaking," the woman replied.

"Hi," I said again, then added, "My name's Lizzy. I'm..."

"I know who you are," she interjected quickly, "I'm so glad you called. I was hoping your father would get back to me, but I guess he must be busy," she said.

I was not about to correct her. The last thing I wanted to do was give her a reason to refuse to tell me just what her note had been about.

"I really would feel better discussing things in person.

Do you think you and your father could come to see me sometime?"

"Yes," I said instantly; then, remembering that, as far as my father was concerned, I knew nothing about this woman or her letter, I added, "Well, I could. Dad's really got a lot on, at the moment, what with the new practice and all," I wasn't lying, not really.

"Well, I guess that's ok," she said, after some thought, "When are you free?"

"I could come tonight after school," I said; certain that Jem wouldn't mind taking me over there.

"Around five?" She asked.

"Sure," I replied.

"Great, I'll see you then," she added and gave me her address, before hanging up.

I smiled, happy that she had agreed to see me without my father, but inside I was feeling a little tense; unsure if I could really handle hearing more worrisome news about the house that I was currently calling home.

I wondered if a part of me was trying to find a way out, an excuse, fitting enough to send me back to the safety and familiarity of the small cottage that I had called home, since birth; yet, I felt so ashamed of myself for even thinking such things. After all, how much had my father sacrificed over the years for my mother and me, even losing his job, because he refused to put us second and his career first?

Now that he had a shot at his long-standing dream of owning his own practice; had got the ball rolling, had opened the doors to his first clients, how could I possibly destroy that for him? I loved my father and knew that if I were to leave, he would soon follow suit. He needed me and here I was doing everything possible to create havoc. Was I just like my mother? Was I a drama queen like her?

As I heard the toilet flush, above, I hurriedly shook those thoughts from my head, and even as I did, I knew that I would keep my appointment with Emily, because, as much as I loved my father, as much as I wanted him to be right and the house to be safe, there was just something about Insane Reno that had me on edge; secrets that still lingered, a danger that seemed ever-present, and I was determined to get to the bottom of it.

CHAPTER 26

I sat in the truck, beside Jem, scanning the street numbers.

"This is it," I cried, gazing at a small pink bungalow with a neat, little front garden and low, rounded hedge, enclosing it.

We climbed out of the truck and I smiled at the small pond, beneath the surface of which, bright gold and silver fish, glittered in the sunlight.

I rapped lightly on the front door and smiled, when, almost instantly, it was pulled open by a tall, dark-haired woman, who could only be described as an older version of Morwena, which left both Jem and I, somewhat lost for words.

"You're a Trerise," she said, looking at Jem, with distrust.

"Are you?" He asked, simply.

"I'll see you; but, not him," she said, ignoring Jem's question.

I looked at Jem; but, he just shrugged.

"I won't be long," I promised, then followed her into the house; noting that Jem's eyes were still, firmly locked on her, as she closed the door behind us.

"I should have guessed they'd have already sunk their claws in," she whispered, as if afraid Jem could still hear her.

"Never takes them long," she added, angrily, as she led me down a neat little hall and into a small kitchen that was modern and clean.

"Please take a seat," she said, indicating the chairs around the table.

"Would you like a drink?" she enquired, once I was seated.

"No thank you."

"You shouldn't trust the Trerises," she said, dropping down into a chair and gazing across at me, "They're not all bad, my brother most certainly isn't," she added, "but, some of them; well, my father, mainly, are really not to be trusted. You see, he wants your house very badly; always has, and I know this must seem slightly crazy, but if you bear with me, I do intend to explain," she said, searching frantically through her pockets, before standing up and retrieving a packet of cigarettes, from the sideboard.

"I hope you don't mind," she said, and I shook my head. I was used to Calvin smoking around me and it was her house. It was up to her what she did, "It's a bad habit, but it helps me to relax," she said, as if ashamed of it.

"My father," she said, frowning, as if the words tasted bad in her mouth, "is a strong man, who, when he sets his sights on something, simply refuses to let go.

I am assuming that man with you is my brother's son. I'd heard he has two, and a daughter, now," she said.

"Morwena," I said, "She looks an awful lot like you."

"Well, my brother is ok. I know you don't have to fear him or his wife;" she said, ignoring my comment about Morwena, "however, I really couldn't comment on his sons or his daughter, for that matter."

I watched her take a long drag on her fag, as she gazed past me and out of the window; seemingly, deep in thought.

"I have avoided anything to do with my father for a long time. It's hard to think of it all again, so please bear with me," she said, pausing; a small sigh, escaping her lips.

"You see, my father believes; whether rightly so or not, that the house you're now living in was built by our ancestors and that they were swindled out of it. I'm not sure of the finer details and they're really not relevant; but, from the things I can remember him telling me, it sounded as if they had simply got into debt and lost it through their own stupidity.

Insane Reno, of course, is a much nicer house, with what is certainly a better location than the home my family now has and my father is desperate to have it back, so much so that when Matthew owned it; dear, sweet, Matthew," she added, a tear in her eyes, "he instigated me to try to get it back into the family."

I listened with rapt attention; knowing, now, that this must be the aunt that Jem had spoken of. I was also intrigued to find out exactly what her father had done to try and get the house back. A part of me wondered if she was about to admit that her father had killed those people, although I found it hard to believe. From what I had seen of him, he appeared to be a nice man; genuine, kind, and helpful, not the sort, who would murder so many people. I watched, as she ran the tip of her cigarette, around the edge of her ashtray slowly and methodically, making the ash taper into a point.

"I was young only fifteen, when he first came to me for my help. I was dating Matthew at the time. It wasn't yet anything special. We had simply been on a couple of dates, which, to be fair, had hardly been raving successes. To be honest, it had always felt very awkward between Matthew and myself; neither of us, really knowing what to say to each other or how to act. You see, Matthew and I had been friends for a long time. Stepping out of that and into dating seemed unnatural and I'm not even sure what possessed us to attempt it," she said, glancing at the clock, and then stubbing her fag out in the ashtray.

"My father, however, was over the moon, at the news, and he came to me and talked about how important it was that I was nice to Matthew; loving and kind. He said that Matthew was a good man and that he was the sort of man I should marry. He was excited; talked about the house, where Matthew lived, saying that, at last, it would be coming back to us. I was confused, but I said nothing. It was nice to see my father, happy."

"Is this the same Matthew that was murdered at Insane Reno?" I asked, wanting to clarify that it was indeed the man, who eventually married my mother's aunt.

"Yes," she said simply, then continued.

"Well, I did as my father asked, but still I could feel that Matthew wasn't into me in that way or me him, for that matter; however, when I tried to explain to my father that I felt Matthew and I were better off as friends, he got mad, very mad. He told me that I had to change Matthew's mind and said that I was to bring Matthew to our house one night and that he would have a talk with him.

I had no idea what he intended to do, but he sent my brother out for the night. My mother had already passed away by this point, so it was just the three of us and my father instructed me to stay in my room, until he called for me.

I could hear them talking downstairs for many hours; was even relieved, when I heard laughter, thinking that they were getting on well and that my father had not said anything hurtful to Matthew, which was a great relief to me, as I cared deeply about him, even if it wasn't really in the way my father wanted it to be.

Around midnight, my father came up to my room and sat on my bed. I could smell the alcohol on him, but said nothing. A part of me I guess, hoped that my father had used the time to talk to Matthew and had learned that, like me, Matthew felt we were better as friends.

Instead, my father said that Matthew would be staying

the night and that he wanted me to sneak into Matthew's room, once he'd had time to settle in, and make love to him.

I was mortified. I'd never had sex before and I had wanted my first time to be with someone I loved; but, my father was insistent and so I agreed and am ashamed to say, did as my father asked.

When I went to Matthew's room, he was sat up on the bed and seemed happy to see me; but, as soon as he spoke, it was clear, he was very drunk.

He asked me to come and sit on the bed with him and I did. I was nervous and unsure how to proceed; but, heeding my father's advice to simply kiss Matthew, that was what I did.

As I'm sure you can see the whole affair was a disaster from start to finish. Neither of us knew what we were doing. I was very afraid and Matthew was very drunk. It is a wonder that he was even able to achieve a state of arousal that would allow him to perform; however he did and, like most men, once Matthew had a taste of sex, he wanted more.

Our relationship changed dramatically, then. Matthew seemed into me, but I was certain it was for all the wrong reasons. His attitude towards me changed, also. It's hard to explain, but it was as if he had lost his respect for me. Before, he had been very protective of me; had looked on me, I think, as innocent, and after I had given myself to him, that stopped. Where, before, he had objected if people cursed around me, he now seemed oblivious to it and, in truth, this hurt me a little; more so than it perhaps should have.

When it came to sex, I often expressed my concerns at falling pregnant; Matthew, however, would reel off reasons why this was unlikely, then, one night, I discovered where he had got these ideas from and it was little surprise, when I discovered that it was my own father.

I, of course, had naively trusted what Matthew said, believing this to be things he had heard from reliable sources; however, on hearing that it was actually my father who had given him this information, I instantly put a stop to our escapades.

I did not trust my father, even then, for he would constantly ask about my and Matthew's relationship; often more interested in whether we were having sex, than if we were falling in love, but by then it was too late," she said, tears forming in the corner of her eyes, as she reached for another cigarette, "I was already pregnant," she cried, lighting the fag, with shaky hands, before continuing.

"My father, of course, was the first to notice the signs. He instantly started talking about how Matthew would have to marry me now; saying that it was the right thing to do.

He was happy, overjoyed in fact, and said instantly that he had to go and look at his house," she continued, emphasising the word his, "It was then that I realised just how stupid we had been," she explained, "The greed in his eyes was clear for all to see and it was then that I truly understood that he had no interest in me or Matthew; he simply wanted that house.

The next day I turned to a friend's mother; Jenny's mother, as it goes."

"Jem's mum?" I asked, and she looked at me perplexed, "Your brother's wife?" I added for clarification.

"Yes," she said simply, then took a deep drag on her cigarette.

"Jenny is very like her mother. Her mother was smart and bold and, when I went to her and told her everything, she was kind to me, and thoughtful.

She told me I was not to worry. She said that she knew someone, who could fix everything and that I would be able to carry on my life as normal.

She was not strictly right; but, she could not have

predicted what would happen and so she arranged for me to have an abortion.

Things were different back then and on the moors we were behind somewhat. The abortion she arranged for me was not one performed by a professional, but by an old lady with a knitting needle.

It was a painful experience and when I returned home and confessed to my father what I had done, for I was in terrible pain, he was mad, but said that it was not a problem. He was sure Matthew would be able to get me pregnant again at a later date.

I was distraught. However, it was not to be the case. I developed an infection and when my father rushed me for medical treatment, I was told that it was unlikely that I would be able to have children in the future. You see, the infection had made me infertile. This news was too much for my father and he hurriedly banished me to my room and later from my home," she let out a long sigh at this and got to her feet.

I was not sure what she was trying to tell me and I was afraid that she was suggesting her father had been responsible for all those murders, but I still just couldn't see it. The man she had just described to me did not seem like the man I had met; but then, I did not know him very well and had only spoken with him on a few occasions. My curiosity getting the better of me, I had to ask, "Are you saying that your father and not Reno killed all those people?"

"No!" She said, spinning round quickly, "God no, I would never suggest that," she said, then paused, her eyes dropping to the floor, "but neither can I say that I have not thought it," she added, her eyes meeting mine, "It was a long time after all this that Matthew's family was killed. If it were my father, I would have assumed that he would have done it sooner; closer to when I disappointed him, but still, my father is a smart man," she added, letting the implication of her words hang in the air.

"All I'm saying is, be careful. Maybe my father will try to push one of his grandsons onto you, as he tried to push me on Matthew. Just be smart, okay?" She said calmly.

I thought of Jem, then. Things had been happening so fast with him. Was Jem secretly doing what his grandfather asked of him? Was I simply a means to get back the farm that had once been theirs; and what of the feud between Tristan and him? Was this because of the house as well?

CHAPTER 27

"So, who is she?" Jem asked, as we drove home, "Is she my banished aunt? I mean, it was like looking at Morwena, forty odd years from now," he said.

"No, I don't think she's your aunt," I lied. How could I tell him the truth, tell him all the things that she had said.

"She was a nut," I said, "She went on and on about the house being dangerous. It was like listening to my mother, all over again. To be honest, I think she's just a lonely, old woman, who's read up on the happenings at the farm, and decided she'd use that knowledge to try and get some company."

"Maybe she's related to mum in some way. I know her dad was a bit of a bugger when it came to the ladies," he said; letting it go to my relief.

"Perhaps," I replied, gazing out of the window.

"Well, it would explain how she knew I was a Trerise and why she didn't want me in the house. Maybe she was resentful of mum, 'cause mum got to have her dad around and she didn't."

"Probably," I replied, simply.

"She hasn't scared you, has she, Tiz?" He asked.

"No," I said, "My heads just a jumble at the moment; exams, you know."

"Not really," he responded, with a smile, "but I didn't

care enough about them, when I was your age, to let them get on top of me. Don't need 'em for what I do anyway," he added.

I watched him out of the corner of my eye as he drove. Was he really just using me? I had always thought of Jem as a nice guy, a bit of a joker, but still nice. Now, I was so confused. Part of me wanted to confront him; call him on it, but the other part was worried. What if his grandfather really was a killer? Would my father and I be next if I rejected Jem? It didn't bear thinking about. I had to find out more; but, how?

"Bet your pup's gonna be glad to see you," Jem said, breaking the silence, "When I let him out earlier he was running around the front garden like a maniac; round the well, over to the gate, all around the edge, determined to find you, he was, then he slumped down in the middle of the path and started whining. Still, he'll get used to it with time," he added.

But, even my beautiful puppy could not draw my attention away from all I had just heard. I needed answers and I was determined that, somehow, I would get them, even if it meant going to see my mother.

CHAPTER 28

At lunch, the next day, I abandoned Calvin, at the school gate; simply telling him there was somewhere I had to go and then hurried off towards my mother's house.

My mum, I knew, would be less than pleased to see me if she thought I was bunking off school, so I had already thought through my excuses and settled on the free study period option.

As for my teachers, a fake note explaining that I had a dentist appointment, followed by my father's faked signature had done the trick.

I'd also arranged for Jem to pick me up, later than normal, down by the triangle, so that I would not have to risk bumping into one of my teachers, back at the school gates.

I was as prepared as I could be; even going so far, as to write down everything I wanted to ask my mother the night before, and then reading them over repeatedly, in order to help me commit each question to memory.

It was these questions that I was now running over silently in my head, as I walked; simply playing around with the wording and trying to plan the best method of attack.

I hadn't seen my mum, since she'd left, as I had refused to go with my father, whenever he'd asked if I would like to join him for a trip into Bude. The reason for me refusing was that he would always head for mum's, before returning home and, although he claimed it was simply to make sure she was ok and didn't need anything, I knew it was really because of how much he still cared for her.

I didn't think mum deserved his visits or his concern; but, what I hated most about dad's trips to see mum was his refusal to call ahead and make sure she was free to talk. It was almost as if he wanted to bump into Imelda's father, as if he wanted to be hurt, and I just couldn't understand why he would want to do that to himself.

When I reached our old street, I was relieved to see that Mr Thomas' beloved car was not parked outside his house or mum's.

I hurried down the road; pausing at the gate to mum's cottage, so that I could gaze at the perfect garden that was as familiar to me as the back of my own hand. Nothing had changed. The cottage was still immaculate with its little, thatched roof, neat borders, and mum's prized rose bushes, running along either side of the path.

Opening the gate, I hurried to the front door; tapping lightly, before standing back to wait.

It seemed like an age, before I heard the latch sliding back and saw mum peering out at me through the small gap between the door and its frame. Her face seemed somewhat thinner and paler than the last time I had seen her and I was a little shocked by this.

"Tizzy!" She exclaimed; quickly bringing me back to the here and now as she yanked the door open and ushered me inside, "Why didn't you call and let me know you were coming? I'd have had your lunch ready, if I'd known," she said, standing up straight and gazing at me, as if she hadn't seen me for months.

"I had some free periods for study, so I thought I would just pop by," I said, turning away from her gaze, as I used my pre-planned lie; however, her normal ability to detect, even the tiniest of lies, seemed not to be working today.

"I've been worried about you," she said, ushering me into a seat and rushing to put the kettle on, "You hardly call and when you do... well, it doesn't matter; I understand you're mad at me."

"Why did you do it?" I asked

"I loved your father very much," she said; her use of love, in the past tense, stabbing at my heart, "but things change, people change," she said, choosing her words carefully.

"You changed, not dad," I said, unable to stop myself, "but I'm not here to talk about that or your affair," I spat, "I'm here to talk about Insane Reno," she froze at this; the spoon she had been using to stir the tea, freezing, mid-spin.

"I have nothing to say about that," she said, bluntly, and I noted that she didn't try to deny her affair with Imelda's father.

"I know you were there for the last murder and I know you had a brother, called Tom, who was killed. What I don't know is what exactly happened that night; because, apparently, you have never talked about it and I want to know, need to know," I added, desperately, "Did the Trerise family have something to do with it?" I hissed, when she didn't respond.

"Reno did it; he killed my family. There's really nothing else to say, Lizzy," she snapped, angrily.

"That's not what you implied that day, in the car, at the farm. You pointed at Jem's grandfather and said he had brought you back. What did you mean?"

"Leave it, Lizzy. I haven't seen you for over two weeks. I don't want to fight."

"I need you to tell me what happened. You say you're concerned about me living there; but, if you're so concerned, then why won't you talk to me? Don't you want me to be prepared, mum?"

"If you come home, you won't have to be prepared!" She snarled.

"This isn't my home. It was never my home, or dad's, for that matter, it was always yours. Everything has always been about what you wanted, until now, at any rate, and that's only because dad stood up to you for once; not that it did him any good, not really. You just jumped straight into bed with Mr Thomas or were you already doing that behind dad's back?" I hissed, then hurriedly held up my hands and snapped, "Don't answer that, I don't want to know. It doesn't matter anyway; just like dad and I never mattered."

"That's not true," she cried, "You always mattered, both of you; but, when your father tried to drag me back there, I just couldn't do it, Lizzy. I knew it was going to happen. Your father's wanted to move back to the moors for years. He'd go on and on about it all the time. He just doesn't understand the curse that rests over that place. It's like there's a hangman's noose, just waiting to strangle whoever enters. You're just like your father, Lizzy; you always were. Both of you are just so infuriatingly stubborn; you just can't understand that I'm trying to protect you."

"From what?" I snapped, "You just said that Reno did it and he's gone isn't he, so what can you possibly need to protect us from?" "Stop it!" She snapped, "For once in your life, just do what I say, please," she pleaded.

"I just want to know what happened. Why won't you tell me anything? I'm not a child anymore, mum."

"I know you're not," she hissed, "but you're not an adult, either, and you wouldn't understand; no one can."

"Try me," I spat, glaring at her.

"Just get out!" She snapped, flying at me and grabbing me by the arm, "Get out of my house and don't come back," she cried, tears streaming down her face, "I can't take any more of this; I couldn't take it from your father and I won't take it from you. I love you, but I won't be abused in my own home like this."

"If you do this, I'll never come back!" I screamed, yanking myself free of her, "I'll never come back and I will never talk to you again!" I spat, my anger bursting forth.

"Then don't!" She hissed, pushing me into the hall and slamming the door.

"Fine!" I screamed, "You call yourself a mother?" I yelled at the kitchen door, behind which she now hid, "You're no mother, you're a monster. I hate you!" I snarled, as I charged for the front door, yanking it open, "You're dead to me!" I cried, storming out and slamming it shut, with as much force as I could muster; certain I would never again have anything to do with her.

CHAPTER 29

I had been wandering aimlessly for over an hour, when I found myself, high up on the cliffs overlooking Crooklets beach. I stood there, gazing out to sea; my head awash with questions like never before.

I just couldn't understand why she refused to talk about it, or that she could be so determined not to, that she was even willing to lose her only child from her life, rather than try and because of this, she was causing a hate to grow inside me that was so strong that I was afraid I would collapse under the weight of it. There was only one person I knew, who seemed willing to discuss anything with me, Emily.

*

I knocked lightly on Emily's door and waited, nervously fiddling with my necklace. I was about to give up hope, when Emily finally appeared, wrapped in a dressing gown; her hair, knotted in a towel.

"I'm sorry. I didn't mean to interrupt you," I said; and then, unable to control myself, I burst into tears.

"Oh my; has something happened?" She asked, ushering me into the house and hurriedly closing the door behind me.

I tried to explain what had happened between my mum and me, but I just couldn't get the words out.

"Come and sit down," she said, gently guiding me into her living room, which, like her kitchen, was modern and very small.

As soon as I was seated, a soft, wet nose pressed into my hand and I found myself gazing down into two large, brown eyes, surrounded by a mop of golden fur.

"That's Ben. Don't mind him," she said, as I gently stroked his silky smooth fur, my fingers running down his large, floppy ears, "He's a cocker spaniel," she said, and then added, "but you probably know that; what with your father being a vet and all. I'd have introduced you to him yesterday, only he was out with his dog walker."

I smiled through my tears.

"Has something happened?" She tried again.

"I'm sorry. I shouldn't have disturbed you; I just didn't know where else to go," I said, feeling a desperate need to explain, but not sure if I really should, "I wanted to call Jem, but I don't know if I can trust him, now," I said; and then, as she rested a hand lightly on my arm, as way of reassurance, I felt certain that she was the person to help me, and so I told her everything; about the house, my mum, and my experiences of the Trerises, so far.

"Well, I'm afraid I don't know anything much about your mother's story. I was long gone by then. Of course, I read the reports in the paper, but I'm over sixty now; my memory is not what it used to be."

I was shocked to hear she was so old; but, of course, when you did the maths it was obvious, yet she looked, as if she was in her forties.

"When you have no one but yourself to take care of," she said, clearly noticing my shocked expression, "it is easy to keep your looks," she added, with a smile, "No stress, you see."

I nodded, and then asked nervously, "Do you really

think your dad could have killed all those people?"

"I don't know; but then, I cannot imagine Reno being responsible for it, either. He had problems, of course, but he was so like a child. I just can't see him being able to do something so cruel; but then, I guess we can never truly know what people are capable of. You hear of people snapping and doing terrible things that they normally wouldn't; sometimes for the strangest of reasons. Perhaps we are all capable of committing murder; just, most of us are never triggered to do it," she paused, as if deep in thought, and then added, "I used to visit him, you know."

"Really?" I asked.

"Yes. He was in a mental health hospital, near Bodmin. They treated him relatively well and he seemed happy, but you couldn't talk to him about the murders. He'd clam up or get upset; much like your mother, I guess."

"Do you think maybe someone had threatened them to scare them into keeping quiet?" I asked, however, my mum was no wimp. I had seen her stand up for herself, on more than one occasion, and she always did it, without any fear; but those people hadn't threatened her life and maybe this person had.

"Perhaps," Emily replied, "pulling a cigarette out and lighting it calmly, "Chances are we will never know; but, you should be careful, because, if Reno wasn't the culprit, then the real murderer may still be out there. I really don't want to scare you Lizzy; but I think, considering the circumstances, it is better for you to be a little nervous and thus, more cautious, than it would be for me to simply lie to you to save you from worry."

I nodded, wiping my eyes carefully, my tears, nearly stemmed, but something was nagging at me and then I realised what it was. When Emily had referred to Reno, it had been in the past tense.

"Do you think, maybe you could get me in to see Reno?" I asked, hoping the past tense way, she had spoken of him, had simply been due to her not seeing him, for a long time; but, when she looked at me, there was sadness in her eyes, and I knew that Reno was no more.

"He died, Lizzy; almost two years ago, now. I was there with him, when he died; it was all very peaceful. I know people might think it was wrong for me to go and hold his hand, like that; but, I almost felt, as if I owed it to Matthew. You see, he never truly believed that Reno had killed his parents, and I, of course, had my own doubts about him killing Matthew and his family. I guess I just felt that, if he was innocent, someone should be there, when he needed them to make up for the injustice, you know."

I nodded, but I couldn't help feeling disappointed. Reno, it seemed, was my only hope of getting answers and now he was gone. If Matthew had been right about Reno and he really hadn't been capable of murder, then there was every chance that the real killer was still out there; just waiting to strike again and, if so, dad and I would be right in the firing line.

CHAPTER 30

I sat alone in my room that night, jotting down everything that had happened, in my diary.

All I knew for sure was that mum and Reno had been the only surviving witnesses of these murders; Reno for all of them and mum for just one. Both had refused to talk about the last murder. Reno, perhaps, had never talked about any of the murders and consequently had taken all he knew to the grave with him. There was the possibility of there being a third witness; the real murderer, if it truly wasn't Reno who had committed these terrible crimes.

Thinking back over everything, once again, I couldn't help but wonder why mum and Reno had refused to talk? Perhaps Reno had threatened my mum into silence or maybe someone else had threatened them both. This however, brought me back to that same question again; if it wasn't Reno, then who?

I had two suspects, so far. That isn't to say there wasn't a chance that there were others, but they were the two that had become apparent; one of them now dead and one a very old man. Reno, of course, had been suffering from Down's syndrome, which made it hard to accurately say whether or not he was even capable of such crimes. Jem's grandfather, as far as I was aware, had been healthy and I would imagine, older than Reno, too, if he was working here as a farmhand at the time of the first murders.

Still, I had to remember that the police, at the time of the last murders, had deemed Reno perfectly able to commit not just one murder, but several; otherwise, surely they wouldn't have sent him to prison. Of course, you did hear of dodgy cops, setting people up in order to save face. Maybe Reno had simply been a way for them to, at last, put the case to rest; after all, he had refused to talk, and what with him being found, clinging to my mother, covered in the victim's blood, perhaps he was just too good a scapegoat for them to resist.

I was not the first person to suspect Reno's innocence; however, as in many of the rumours that flew around about the murders, a large number of people had argued over his ability to be able to take so many lives without being caught. This was something I could relate to; because surely, Reno would have always been a suspect. The first murder, it might have been brushed off; Reno, having been young and, in many people's eyes, unable to do it. By the second, I'm sure people would have been starting to wonder; not to mention the fact that Matthew had been forced to fight to keep Reno from going to prison, so I knew the cops had wanted him charged for the murders, even then. It's not surprising; after all, Reno had been the only survivor twice.

Then, of course, you had to bear in mind Matthew; a man, who had known Reno so well and had, himself, believed Reno incapable of such crimes. Surely, if he'd had any doubt about Reno's innocence, he'd have been the first to send him off to prison, especially as his own parents were two of the murder victims; yet, Matthew had not even doubted Reno for a second and had, in fact, fought hard to keep Reno from being charged for the murders.

My mother, however, seemed to have no qualms about Reno going to prison, nor had she made any effort to visit him since the murders, as far as I knew; but why? Surely, if he were innocent, she'd have said so. After all, dad had said that she and Reno were incredibly close. Would my mother have been so desperate to protect herself that she'd let an innocent man go to prison, regardless of whether she cared about him or not?

I wanted to believe that if she really had sent an innocent man off to prison, she did so because she was protecting him. After all, if she knew the murderer was still out there, she may very well have been afraid that he would strike again and perhaps this had made her desperate to get Reno away from the farm. Could she really have done that, if he hadn't been forcibly removed?

The problem was Jem's grandfather, still kept popping into my head. Surely, he must have been a suspect in the past, as well. He was, after all, living at the farm, even if it was out in the barns and not in the actual house. He had also been willing to trick Matthew into sleeping with his young daughter, in order to ensure that she fell pregnant and that Matthew would be forced to marry her, thus bringing the farm back into his family. Was he also capable of killing to get the same result? Surely, these things must have come up. Matthew must have thought about this himself, when he was trying to keep Reno out of prison. But, if that really were the case, then why had Matthew allowed Derek to continue to work at the farm, or had he? I wasn't actually sure, when Derek had stopped working at the farm and, if he had been let off or even left himself, after the second murders, then perhaps, when the third murders took place, he'd seemed much less of a suspect. With only Reno left it may have made things seem even more clear-cut to the police involved in investigating the murders; but, would it really have wiped Derek off of the suspect list, once and for all? After all, his own family's farm really wasn't that far away.

Admittedly, Reno being found covered in the victim's

blood would have swung the attention away from Derek a fair amount; but, with Reno's Down's syndrome, it wasn't hard to see that he might have rushed to the victims and held them close in his distress, without even considering the consequences of such actions.

The problem with the idea of Derek being the true murderer was the question of why he would leave Mum and Matthew alive, when he'd killed the rest of their families.

With Reno, it seemed obvious; because he would surely want someone he trusted to continue to take care of him and in both cases he had left people that he was very close to alive, but with Derek, it was not so clear cut. After all, one of the ways to get the house was to take over Reno's care. By leaving Matthew alive, he had left someone who was not only old enough to take on that responsibility, but also clearly would have been next of kin and thus, would be guaranteed to inherit the farm and the job of caring for Reno, which would mean Derek would simply be left with the same problems that he had been faced with before. If Derek was responsible for these murders, he must have realised that by leaving Matthew alive there was going to be a risk that he would be forced to kill, once more.

Perhaps he had believed that he could get Matthew with his daughter again; but, that would be crazy. By that point, he had already banished his daughter. It was hardly likely he would be able to bring her back for attempt two. Maybe he had believed Matthew would shy away from the farm, as my mother had. After all, few people would be able to cope with living in a place, where their family had been killed, so terribly; and, if that had been the case, he may have believed that he could offer Matthew a fair or not so fair price for the farm and gain it in that fashion.

Unable to figure out what Derek's motives may have been for leaving Matthew alive, I decided to look at why he might have done the same with my mother. With mum it was a lot easier to figure out Derek's possible reasoning behind leaving her alive. After all, she was a girl and if he took over her care after the murders, as he had clearly tried to, then he could easily marry her off to his son, when she was older, or possibly even adopt her into his own family. However, mum had ruined any hope of that, when she refused to live with him and had done her best to avoid him at all costs. Had she really only done that because he tried to get her to open up about the final murders or had she done it because she knew he was the culprit. If it was the latter, it would also explain why Derek was really so keen to push her to open up.

Perhaps, he was not really worried about her well-being, but worried for his own. After all, mum had been in the house the night of the murders. If he had been the true murderer, there was a chance that she had seen him. Her reaction to him would certainly suggest that she had. That, surely, would have caused him concern and would hardly be the sort of thing a murderer would want to leave hanging around if he were uncertain; essentially, it would have been like having a ticking time bomb hanging about his neck.

The problem was, things were a lot clearer, if you looked at it with Reno as the murderer. On both occasions, he had left someone he was close to within the family, alive; probably in the hope that they would continue to take care of him. However, as hard as I tried, I just couldn't figure out a motive for him wanting to kill the others. I had read and heard several theories, but none of them really added up. Most of them revolved around the house. But, if my dad was right, when he said that Reno's father had left the farm to the first murder victims, on the condition that Reno be cared for within the house until his death, then why would Reno need to kill?

My head was reeling. There were so many possibilities; but, it was clear, when you looked at it closely, that the only true culprit could be Reno. If someone else had wanted the house, they would have killed all the family members, each time; probably then offering themselves up as potential carers for Reno. They would not have left people alive, who could then go on to inherit the house.

Ok, so in mum's case, she was young enough to need a carer, herself, and Jem's grandfather had offered that service, along with my father's parents; but, Matthew had been more than old enough to care for himself, when his parents were killed, and so the offer from Jem's grandfather had to be taken for what it clearly was; just genuine kindness. Yes, later he had pestered mum to talk; but, as he had worked here as a farm hand for years, he had clearly been very close to all the people that had been killed here and, bearing that in mind, he would no doubt have been desperate to know what had happened that night and all the other nights that Reno had set about wiping out those that cared for him. On top of that, as my dad had said, Derek had probably believed that it was unhealthy for my mother to keep it all locked inside, as did I.

I could not justify what the grandfather had tried to do with Matthew and his daughter, but we all make mistakes. Had it happened after Matthew's parents' death, then maybe I would have had more reason for suspicion; but, from what Emily had said, I knew that was not the case and for that reason it was simpler to just let it go.

I could sit here and worry about Jem as much as I wanted, but the truth was I could not believe him capable of simply dating me to get his hands on this farm. Maybe I was simply deluding myself or perhaps I was right; the reality was I might never know, but I couldn't continue to worry about these things, not with my exams looming.

Slamming my diary shut, I stretched out on my bed and sighed.

It was over. Reno had killed those people, no one else,

and it was time to let it go.

CHAPTER 31

Two months had passed since I had decided to drop my quest to figure out the true happenings at Insane Reno and move on. I had wiped mum from my life, completely; despite my father begging me to reconsider. Jem and I were officially dating. Bailey was now, fully inoculated and my exams were going well with only a few remaining, which had left me happily looking forward to the summer holidays.

My life revolved around the farm, my father, Jem and the animals, and it suited me, perfectly. Jem had been great, helping me with my revision: often riding with me on the moors, a book in one hand, the reins of his beautiful bay gelding in the other, as he tested my knowledge, while at the same time helping me learn my way around the moors, which, to my father's delight, had now, fully captured my heart.

It is hard to explain the moors to those who have never fully experienced them; but, for me, the moors held a magic and intrigue like no other place I had ever known. It was full of interesting history, hidden secrets, and dark tales of love, lust, and fear.

As Jem led me over the moors, he talked to me of ghosts, murders, and days gone by; showing me old farm houses, abandoned and disused, as well as the outline of old settlements that seemed to be dotted all around the Tors. It seemed there was nothing Jem did not know about the moors that he so clearly adored.

There was Charlotte Dymond, the poor girl believed to have been murdered by her boyfriend, Matthew Weeks; the anniversary of her death, drawing many to Rough Tor, in hopes of seeing her ghost, who has frequently been spotted wandering the moors nearby. Her unrest, it is believed, is due to her real murderer going unpunished as many think Matthew Weeks was wrongly accused of murdering Charlotte; a crime he was later hung for.

Then there was the Lady of the Lake, believed to reside in Dozmary pool, which was once believed to be bottomless, until droughts in 1859 and 1976 proved otherwise.

Back when Dozmary pool was believed to be bottomless, another well-known figure played a part in the lake's history. His name was Jan Tregeagle, a very evil man, who was set the impossible task of emptying the pool of water, using only a limpet shell, in which there was a hole; a task that would, supposedly, protect him from the hounds of hell, until his judgement day.

Then, of course, you had the very well-known tales, such as the famous Beast of Bodmin Moor; a large black panther that was reported to have been sighted many times by countless people and the famous Jamaica Inn, with its smuggling past and ghostly goings on, as well as it's connection to the famous author, Daphne Du Maurier, whose books I had been devouring with delight.

I relished all these tales and more, scanning the internet and books, desperate to learn as much as possible about the moors that had become so important to me; however, I was doubtful that my own knowledge could ever hope to be as vast as Jem's, for it seemed there was nothing he did not know.

Through my time with Jem, out riding on the moors, I

learnt that the story which fascinated him the most was that of Charlotte Dymond. He discussed her tale in great detail, running over the circumstances believed to have led up to her death, as well as Matthew's wrongful arrest; arguing Matthew's innocence, as if he had known the man, personally. He was adamant that the memorial that sat at the base of Rough Tor, clearly stating that Matthew had been Charlotte's murderer, was merely an attempt for the true killer's family to further convince others of the lie they had concocted, in order to protect their own. It was an interesting topic and I loved hearing him talking animatedly about things that clearly, were of immense interest to him.

The farm; Jem's other passion, which he shared with my father, was also going well. While Dad worked hard in the practice, building relationships with our ever-growing clientele that would see them remain loyal to us for life, Jem had set about building up the livestock and we now had a small herd of sheep and some highland cattle; huge, hairy beasts with great big horns, just like those I had seen roaming the moorland roads, nearby.

The move had been a complete success and all of the ghostly goings-on, seemed to have drawn to a halt. On top of this, the cottage in Bude was under offer; meaning, soon my father would be able to pay off the loan he had taken out in order to renovate the farm. Mum had chosen to simply walk away from the lot. She had moved fast, too; divorce papers, landing on the mat, almost a month ago. The final heartache for my father would come, once all was finalised; but, he was coping with it as he did everything in life, simply acting, as if all was fine and taking each day one step at a time.

Imelda, however, was still doing her best to irritate me at school; telling me how well mum had settled into their home and how much she enjoyed having a mother figure in her life, again. Although, at first, this had inflamed my anger greatly, I now simply let it wash over me; reminding myself that my mum had done her best to destroy our family and that she had failed. Imelda was welcome to her.

*

It was a beautiful sunny day. Morwena and I were out riding near Rough Tor, when she turned to me and said, "I'm so excited about you and Jem. I mean, just imagine it; you becoming a Trerise, our family empire, growing. Just think, the Trerise family will own one of the best and worst farms on the moors. Now, how many families can claim that, aye?"

I gazed across at her then, my mind working overtime, and pulled Misty to a halt.

"It'll be my father's farm," I said, eyeing her, cautiously.

"Yeah, I know; but, you're gonna inherit it one day, aren't you, and you'll probably be a Trerise by then," she said, stopping her horse and smiling across at me.

"And then, it will be my farm," I growled.

"So, you're not going to share with Jem, then?" She asked, perplexed; the smile, fading from her face.

"Of course I am," I snapped, "but ultimately, it will be mine, just as your farm will be his."

"Well, maybe granddad won't leave our farm to him," she snapped, "Maybe he'll leave it to me and Tristan."

"Jem's the oldest," I hissed, not sure why I even cared, "Anyway, everyone knows our farm is better than yours. Why else would your grandfather have wanted it so bad that he would banish his own daughter, when she refused to go along with his plot to trick Matthew Yelland into marrying her?"

"What are you on about?" Morwena cried, looking genuinely shocked. "My grandfather did no such thing. He was angry at her for having an abortion, that's all."

"Whatever!" I snarled back.

"My granddad liked Matthew. He even helped him, when he first took over your farm. He helped everyone that had your farm, even your dad. He didn't have to, but he did," she yelled, yanking her horse around and kicking it into a gallop.

And then it hit me, her grandfather had gone out of his way to help everyone, including my father. He had immersed himself into the world of all who owned the house. Would a farm hand really keep coming back like that after so many murders; especially when he had no need to? Derek certainly had not needed to keep working at Reno, because he'd inherited his own family's farm and, from Morwena's words, it was clear that the Trerise family were completely over the moon at the prospect of gaining Insane Reno, back into their family. Was Derek finally getting what he had wanted all along?

I turned Misty around and rode her, hard, back to the farm.

Jem emerged from the barn, as I entered the yard, and smiled up at me, "Hello, beautiful," he said; then seeing my flushed expression, he asked, "Is everything ok?"

"Why did your granddad work here, instead of on his own family's farm?" I asked.

Jem looked at me, perplexed, as he rubbed his hands clean with a tatty old rag and gazed up at me, "Why the sudden interest?" He asked.

"Just tell me!" I snapped, angrily.

Tucking the rag in his pocket, Jem folded his arms and shook his head, clearly displeased at my tone, and said, "He was trying to secure a future for himself. He had an older brother, who was going to inherit our farm, so he wanted to have work of his own. He was pretty determined, my granddad; adamant that he was going to earn enough money to buy his own farm, but he didn't need to in the end. His brother died in an accident and my grandfather inherited the lot."

"What sort of accident?" I asked, trying to keep my voice calmer this time.

"He fell off the barn roof and was impaled on some farm machinery. He and my grandfather were up there fixing it and he slipped. Granddad tried to grab him, but he wasn't quick enough. Tiz; what's with all the questions, what's wrong?" He asked firmly.

I jumped off of Misty, hurrying her into the barn and rushed to remove her tack, Jem close on my heels.

"What's going on?" He asked, after watching me for a few minutes.

"I need you to take me into Bude," I said, working as fast as I could.

"Are you gonna tell me why?" He asked, his arms still crossed, as he watched me closely.

"I have to see my mum, but I'll explain everything on the way," I lied, "Just help me get Misty sorted, ok?" I said, thrusting her saddle towards him and doing my best to give him a warm, reassuring smile, while my mind worked overtime.

Was Derek's brother's fall from the barn roof truly another accident or had he been pushed by his own brother; a brother, who had wanted a farm of his own, so badly, that he had lost sight of what was wrong and right?

Had Derek also murdered all those poor people, who had lived at Reno, before me, and then placed the blame on a poor man, suffering from Down's syndrome, who had no hope of defending himself?

But, the biggest question of all; the one that tormented my every breath and kept my heart pounding in panic was simply this, would my father and I be next on his deadly list of destruction?

CHAPTER 32

The drive to mum's was an awkward one and I was relieved, when at last, we pulled up outside. Although, the house was now under offer, mum had not yet moved all her things across to Mr Thomas', and so, according to my father, spent a lot of time in our old house, packing things up. I was hoping she would be there, now. The prospect of knocking at Imelda's door was a less than pleasing one, so it was with some reluctance that I slowly moved towards the front door.

I did not knock, as normally, I would; but instead, used my old key and entered into the hallway, calling out to mum, as I moved from room to room. As I entered the kitchen, I saw mum's large, oak chest; something she had always had and I'd always been forbidden to go near, sat on the table with the top open.

I gazed at it, mystified. The box had always been kept firmly shut and locked, and because of this, it had always held a forbidden temptation for me.

Moving closer, I peered inside and began to sift through the contents; an old blanket, a well-worn teddy bear, a little, wooden horse, and a collection of photos. Reaching inside, I pulled out a handful of the pictures and scanned through them; seeing a girl, not too dissimilar from myself, smiling back. In some, she was accompanied by a young boy, who had short, chocolate hair, in a very similar shade to my mother's and mine, and a sprinkling of freckles across his cute, button nose, and I knew that this must be Tom. In others, she was with an elderly couple that I assumed to be mum's aunt Julie and, of course, Matthew Yelland.

I noted that Matthew was a very large man; but, despite his extensive girth, he seemed quite toned. His skin was tanned in a way that made it hard to tell, whether it was from long days spent out in the hot sun or lack of washing. Yet, despite his scruffy hair, grubby appearance, and huge size, his large, jocular smile gave me the sense that he was every bit as sensitive and caring as people said.

His wife, Julie, was also very large; although, no match for her husband. She was wearing a grubby apron, underneath which could be seen a faded, flowery dress that hung to below her knees. Her chocolate hair had been looped around in a very lopsided bun with strands sticking out in all directions, including two long tendrils that fell, either side of her chubby face. She, too, had a warm, welcoming smile and the large green wellies that encased her feet, and seemed, so out of place, had me chuckling to myself.

Looking down into the box again and sifting more photos out of the way, I came across a small, white book, the cover of which had been decorated with ribbons and pressed flowers.

I eased it slowly out, opened the first page, and began to read...

Dear Diary,

Today, Aunt Julie and I went picking wild flowers, on the moors. It was a beautiful day, the sun was shining, and Tom was out with Uncle Matthew. I like it best, when he is busy, elsewhere; as, when he comes with us, he crushes more flowers, than he picks.

Sadly, Reno was unable to come with us today, as he is very poorly. I ask God, every night, before I go to bed, to help him get better, as I know that Aunt Julie is very concerned for him; even if she does not tell me so.

I sat back, shocked, for I had found my mother's diary; a diary that clearly dated back to her days at Reno. Hurriedly, I flicked through it, desperate to see if it documented the night of the murders and came upon an entry, where the ink was smudged, as if my mother had been crying, when she wrote it. It read...

Dear Diary,

The most terrible thing has happened and I'm so scared; I don't know what to do. My whole family is gone and Reno has been taken away. People keep telling me that he is bad and that I am not to worry about him, anymore; but, I am so scared of what will be done to him and I know that he will not cope, without those he loves, around him. Please, let him be safe. Please, do not let anyone hurt him.

I pray daily for God's guidance and I pray, too, that I was right and did right and hope that, if I was wrong, I'll be forgiven; for I only did what I thought was best and did not mean to be bad.

I am glad to be living with the Bray's, who are very nice to me; but, I am too afraid to tell anyone what happened, because I do not want them to think that I am wicked. I only did what I thought was right and best and I'm afraid, too, because Reno said I'd die, if I ever talked about it.

I wish that I had been killed, too. I wish that I hadn't slid from my bed and hidden, beneath it, like a coward, when I saw that door opening; because, if I had been braver, then I would not be left behind, afraid and ashamed, as I am, now.

I don't feel big enough to carry so much and I don't want to make bad choices; for didn't mummy always say that bad choices would haunt you till the day you die?

I skimmed backwards this time, reading entry after

entry; trying to find something that alluded to the night of the murder, but nothing gave away what had happened that night. She talked about her life with the Yelland's, her brother, and Reno, but did not document the real happenings on the night of the murder; merely alluding to it, from time to time, in later posts.

Skimming forward, once more, and about ready to give up, altogether, I discovered another entry, which started...

Dear Diary,

I told John there was a secret door in my old bedroom, yesterday, and today, he went to the farm to see.

He said he checked the wall in the area that I had told him to look, but could not find a door at all. Still, I know it is there, because I saw the bad man come through it.

I read on, with baited breath, and learned that she intended to go to the farm, herself, in order to search for the hidden door.

Full of nervous anticipation, I flipped forward; first several days, then a week, without finding any further mention of her plan and it was only after I had travelled though several months of her documented life that I found what I was looking for.

Dear Diary,

I went to the house today, alone, because I was worried John might try to stop me, had I told him of my plans, straight off, without having any proof.

I was so scared to be back in that house and I was not prepared for all the memories it would bring back or for how much those memories would hurt; even the good ones.

When I saw some of Tom's old toy soldiers, lying on the floor, I forgot for a moment that he was gone and was certain that, at any minute, Aunt Julie would find them and chastise him for leaving them, right there, in the centre of the hall; where they could easily be stepped on. Then, when I remembered that they were gone, all of them, gone; my aunt, my uncle, Tom, and even Reno, if not quite in the same way, I had to fight back tears, and was certain that at any second, my heart would break from the pain of it.

To go up those stairs was so hard, but I made myself do it, taking each step slowly, avoiding those I knew would creak; although, I was not sure who I feared would hear me.

When I got to my room, I tried so hard to open that secret door; but, although I found a thin line, running down the wall, I could not get anything to fit inside, and despite trying very hard, I failed to move it, by even an inch.

I got very angry, in the end, and I smashed through the door with Tom's old cricket bat, which I'd found in the kitchen. I don't think I have ever been so mad in my whole entire life, not even when my parents died and Tom and I were taken away from all we knew. But, I was very glad of that anger, for it erased all my fear and gave me the strength to do something I never could have imagined possible before.

I was so proud of myself, when I had that door smashed; so bad, I could see through it to the very thin passage, behind, and by poking my head through the hole, I was able to see some stairs, heading down into what seemed a very dark hole.

The darkness of that hole, however, had me scared, all over again, and I could not bring myself to go any further, on my own, and instead, ran to tell John what I had found.

It took forever for me to convince him that I was telling the truth, but thankfully his own curiosity stopped him from going to his parents; for he knew he'd never get to see the secret rooms for himself, if he were to tell.

Still, he did not let us go right there, but instead, insisted we be prepared; asking me all sorts of questions about what I had seen, when I had peered through, so that he could be sure to pack all we would need.

Yanking a pillowcase from his bed, he had crept around the house, packing all he felt we would need. It was only when we had several candles, some matches, and a handful of mixed biscuits, stolen from the cookie jar in the kitchen that he announced we were ready to go.

When we got to the farm, he was much braver, than I, and rushed up to my room, so fast that I struggled to keep up with him; and, though my heart was pounding with fear, I felt much happier for having him there.

Once in my old room, we each lit a candle and then with John in front, we headed down those long, thin, steep stairs; deep into the belly of the house, for that was where we found ourselves, once we reached the bottom of those stairs, or at least, that is how it felt, for we stood in a very small room that John felt sure was hidden, beneath my uncle's little snug. However, this gave me no comfort, for this room did not have the same warm, comforting feel, nor the large, welcoming fireplace.

Instead, it was dark and gloomy, with no windows or natural light of any kind and there were cobwebs in the corners that made my skin crawl.

We found many other rooms beneath the house, most, however, no grown-up could have hoped to walk in; not unless they had failed to grow like that funny little man we saw at the circus, once.

John also found a long tunnel, which we crawled through, until John nearly tumbled out, into the bottom of the well. If I had not grabbed his belt, so fast, I know he would have. And it would have been my fault, too; for I had distracted him, by crying out, when I thought I felt something brush my hand.

When John looked up, he said he could see the top of the well, but no way up and out of it. It was only when he laid on his back and felt around the whole of the tunnel that he found a brick, above, to be missing, and by sliding himself out, further, while I gripped tightly to his feet, he was able to see that there were many bricks missing; all the way up to the top, and by using these slots, we were able to climb up and out of the well, very slowly.

John says, it is clearly a secret entrance into the house and I let him think he was telling me something I didn't know; because, my mother always told me that men like to feel smart and that the best women, always play dumb, in order to allow men's egos to grow strong and healthy, as they should.

At least, I now know how the man got in. Maybe Reno wasn't involved, after all. But, I must never tell, for I promised Reno I never would and I can't break that promise; not when I have already let him down so badly.

I sat back, trying to process what I had just read, and suddenly, things began to click into place.

The murderer hadn't left mum alive through choice or Matthew, for that matter; he needed their room empty to gain access to the house. And, hadn't my dad said that mum was supposed to have stayed at a friend's house that night, but had been collected, because she had grown home-sick. Reno surely would have been aware of her return home; but, the true murderer, not living within the house, probably would have been unaware of that fact.

My room was the room with the hidden door and I had a sneaking suspicion that the door in question was right behind my bed. Why else would the wall be thinner there, than the rest of the house? Maybe Tom's ghost had not been trying to scare me, but show me.

Stuffing everything back in the box, bar mum's diary, I rushed for the front door, full of a new found determination to discover the truth; yet, as I climbed into the truck, beside Jem, both my mother's words and Emily's came back to me and looking at the man I had fallen in love with, I was, once more, filled with fear, wondering if his grandfather was really the true murder and if, even now, Jem was working alongside his grandfather to plot a fourth and perhaps final gruesome massacre.

CHAPTER 33

I spent the next two days reading my mother's diary. She did not say much about what had happened to her the night of the murders; but, there were snippets of information about other aspects of her life that helped me gain a little insight into the kind of person my mother had been, both before and after the murders had taken place.

It was the 14th of April and the anniversary of Charlotte Dymond's death. I had waited patiently for this night, before trying to enter the hidden rooms; knowing that Jem would be off at Rough Tor, in the hopes of spotting the elusive ghost of Charlotte, while my father had, long ago, made plans to go out with friends.

I had already examined the wall, behind my headboard, but I could see no gap and assumed that my father had had the door blocked up; meaning, my only entry into the hidden rooms would be down the well, which I had also investigated and found to be, just as my mother had described.

As the night drew in, Jem tried pestering me into going with him to Rough Tor, but I refused; saying that I had revision to do and when he, at last, climbed into his truck, Beans and Bailey by his side, I breathed a sigh of relief.

I sat down at my computer, brought up some web pages, and laid out some of my books; determined to get a little bit of revision done, so that I would have something to show him, when he returned.

I worked for almost an hour, before it became, too much, and jumping up, I hurried downstairs to find my father's keys.

Night time, on the moors, is so much more intense than it is in Bude. There are no lights, bar the stars and the moon, above, and I was thankful that tonight was clear.

Using the moonlight to guide me, I made my way to the well, clutching my father's keys tightly in my quavering hands. I had never had a problem with small spaces, nor the dark, but the thought of what might lurk, down there, had me somewhat on edge. Still, I took up the large padlock and inserted the key, praying that I would find no bugs waiting, down in the dark.

The lock opened with relative ease, but the heavy grate was so hard to lift that it took several attempts before, at last, I was able to get it up high enough that I could pull it back towards me.

Pulling the torch from my back pocket, I shone it down into the well, checking the positions of my foot holds, before slotting it into my inside pocket for safe-keeping. Easing myself, up over the side, and feeling with my feet for the first set of missing bricks, I began my descent into the darkness.

I moved slowly, cautious of the dampness that lingered on the walls from the heavy downpours, which had been attacking the moors on and off, all day. The small holes that provided me with an easier decent, also had my skin crawling, as regularly, my hands were met with stringy cobwebs; the owners of which I prayed I would not meet.

At last, I felt the larger opening of the tunnel, and by climbing a little further down the well, I was able to slide inside; cobwebs, clinging to my face and hair, as I did so. Trying not to think of giant spiders and other creepy crawlies, I pulled my torch, out of my inside pocket, and shone it around me.

The hole was small, but I would be able to crawl along it, on my hands and knees, with relative ease, and although there were cobwebs lining the outer edges, I was relieved to find that the floor was smooth and dry. As I slowly edged down the tunnel, my torch, held between my lips, I tried only to focus on my progress and not the webs, all around me.

As I moved along, I could feel grooves, beneath my hands, as if something had been dragged along here repeatedly over a long period of time; but, I could see nothing but a brick wall, ahead.

As I drew nearer to this, however, it became apparent that the tunnel turned, and taking the torch from my mouth, I shone it down the new path; seeing that, just ahead of me, it seemed to slope down and grow wider.

I hurried along it, as fast as I could; at last, reaching a point, where I could stand. It was just a small area, with a door at one end and a small, wheeled, wooden trolley, resting to one side that had ropes attached, at both ends. I followed the rope with my eyes, noting that it looped through a pulley system, and I guessed that this was the reason for the grooves I had felt, along the floor of the tunnel; although, I was not altogether sure why something like that would be necessary.

Moving around the trolley, I eased the door open and found myself in a small room, only slightly bigger than the den, in which there were several doors, but no windows. In the middle of the room, sat a small table, on top of which, sat an old book that I was instantly drawn to.

Fingering the book, with its old, tatty cover, I noted that there was no dust on it or for that matter, any of the other surfaces, around the room; clearly someone had been down here, keeping the room clean, but who? And, how had they gained access? It was clear no one had crawled through the tunnel, from the well, for some time.

Opening the book, I found the pages were worn, and in places, coming loose from their binding. The book was clearly some sort of diary, for each page was dated and covered with scruffy writing that was, at times, hard to read. It began like this...

12 may

I have taken a job at the large farm, on the edge of the moors, once owned by my family, and am living in two small rooms, tucked inside the large barn.

As I watch my employers, strutting around; full of gloating pride, I am filled with rage. This farm belongs to my family and to us it should have been left, but I intend to get it back; whatever it takes.

It was signed, Derek Trerise.

I flicked through the book to the last entry and was shocked to see handwriting that was neat and tidy and clearly not written by the same hand as the first entry.

The last entry read...

1 of April 2010

Jem is proving a problem in our plans; although, grandfather seems happy with the new turn of events. He says that Jem's relationship with Tizzy is the best outcome we could have hoped for and that, as long as they marry, the house will be back in the family's name.

I should have tried harder with her after all the ghost stuff, but there is no chance of me getting her away from Jem, now; not unless I take his life, which I fully intend to do. After all, grandfather took his brother's life, didn't he? However, I intend for Jem's to be a much more intricate affair than simply falling from a roof.

There has been little of interest on the cameras and the conversation at the house is boring. I think it might be fun to find a way to liven things up again; although, granddad is against this, feeling that now we should simply let things run their course between Jem and Tizzy. But, I will not let Jem win this and have it all, while I am left with nothing.

Tristan

I glared at the page, shocked. It seemed my suspicion of Derek had been well founded, after all. Tristan had stated clearly that Derek had killed his own brother and now it seemed that Tristan planned to follow in his grandfather's footsteps. So, Jem was innocent in all this; not only innocent, but because of me, he had become a potential victim.

I flicked back through the pages hurriedly, pausing when I came to several, on which photos had been glued; photos that seemed to be of the smoke alarms and electric sockets in our house. I scanned back through the pages, past some diagrams; until, at last, I came to some more text. It read...

At last, all the listening and video devices have been installed. We will be able to monitor everything that happens in the house, twenty-four seven. We have also rigged up some extra little treats, to give the young girl and her mother a few frights.

Hopefully, we will be able to scare the whole family out of the house, relatively quickly, by using these simple devices and will then be able to easily convince John Bray into selling the house to our family, at a considerably lowered price.

I thought back to all the scary things that had happened and looking around me, noticed among other strange equipment dotted around the room, an old CD player. I moved across to it; turning the volume low, before hitting play.

Instantly, voices filled the room; whispering, giggling voices, the very same voices that I had heard that day in the den. Suddenly, my skin was crawling, as I realised that someone had been down here in this room, purposefully trying to scare me.

Determined to know all that had been going on, below our very feet, I moved around the small room; slowly flicking monitors on, as I went. Once all 15 of the small screens were going, I stood back to look at them and was horrified to see that almost every inch of the house and yard were covered; except, to my relief, the bathroom.

A shiver ran up my spine with the realisation that we had been watched, so closely. I desperately tried to think back over everything I had done in the house; cringing at the embarrassing things I may have done, thinking I was unobserved.

Wanting to put the intrusion of our privacy out of my mind, I gazed around me; trying to work out, which wall would be the one, under the den's fireplace, and moved towards the door on the left hand side of it.

Pulling it open, I found a small staircase. Shining my torch, up to the top, I spotted a strange device, on the end of which, was a round tennis ball. Climbing the stairs slowly, I examined the strange machine and instantly knew that I had been duped, again. It had been no ghost, thumping on the wall, behind my bed; just as ghosts hadn't been the cause of the voices in the den. Spotting a button, and wanting to be sure that I was correct in my suspicions, I hit it, and sure enough, the tennis ball began a steady, rhythmic thump, against the wall.

Anger raging inside me, I stopped the machine quickly and hurried down the stairs, flinging open doors. All the rooms, off of the main one, were incredibly low; just as my mum had described in her diary. Behind one door, I found a makeshift bed, behind another, a small fridge, stocked with food; around which, sat a collection of cans and jars.

Rushing back into the small room, I searched for any hidden doors; wondering if perhaps, there was something my mother had missed, but I found nothing.

I knew there had to be a simpler way into the room than the well. It would be incredibly hard for anyone to get into the house, on a regular basis, through it; without drawing attention to themselves, and the cobwebs that lined the tunnel, made it clear that it was disused, which meant there had to be another way in.

I knew the door to my room was blocked off, but... I paused; suddenly, realisation hitting me.

The passage; mum had been afraid of the passage, too. Did she know something I didn't? I rushed back to the stairs, as I knew there was a gap, running down beside them, which I had simply brushed off, before, as it seemed to lead to a dead end. But, I was starting to realise that not everything was what it seemed in this house. After all, I had always assumed the passage was there, simply because of the chimney breasts for the two large fireplaces, when the real reason was to hide the hidden stairs. It was all very clever.

The gap beside the stairs was small, but I was able to pass through it with ease and stand in the thin passage, behind. It seemed that the passage was just an empty space, with no doors, but I noticed there was a metal bar, fixed to the wall, at the far end. I pulled it and pushed it; but, nothing happened. Running my hands, all over, I searched for a secret lock; but again, found nothing.

It was only when I examined the floor that I noticed one of the stone flags was higher than the rest and so I pressed down on it; feeling movement. Standing up, I stepped onto it and gripped the metal bar and tried to pull it and then push. Part of the wall began to move slightly; but, it made a terrible scraping sound and seemed only willing to open outward. I had found what I was looking for; but, I knew I had to be doing something wrong, because, had someone tried to open it, like this, when I was in the house, I would have heard it.

In my frustration, I jumped hard on the stone slab and suddenly the door flew open; something, causing it to stop, before it could hit the wall, on the other side, and make a thud. Gazing out through the opening it had left, I found myself looking at the passage, between our kitchen and the den; just as I had suspected.

Leaving the door open, I quickly ran and retrieved the book; freezing, as I spotted movement on one of the small screens. Moving closer, I froze with horror, as I saw Derek Trerise, slowly creeping out from behind the barn.

Panic gripping me, I rushed for the hidden door, pulling it closed; forgetting the flag stone, in my haste. An ear splitting screech of protest echoed through the house and, coming to my senses, once more, I jumped heavily on the slab, yanking on the bar, so hard that, as the door crashed closed, I tumbled back, onto the unforgiving cold, slab floor. Praying to God to save me, I frantically scurried to my feet and rushed for the secret tunnel; which now seemed my only hope.

As I dashed past the screens, I hurriedly snatched up Derek and Tristan's combined diary and stuffed it, down my top; pausing, only briefly, to scan the screens.

I spotted Derek, leaning through the back door, his head slowly turning, as he surveyed the empty kitchen; suspicion on his face, as he stepped inside.

Once in the tunnel, I scurried along it, as fast as I could, cursing myself for stupidly dropping my torch. The enclosed space and my fear of being caught was causing my chest to tighten; but, I was too afraid to suck in air for fear my breaths would be heard by the old man, who I could now hear calling out, behind me.

"Tristan, are you in here?" he asked, "Is everything ok? Tristan, answer me," he called, perplexed.

I reached the end of the tunnel and quickly pulled the diary out; worried I might drop it in the climb to the top. It was too big to grip between my teeth, as I had done with the torch, but at the same time, I couldn't leave it behind; not when it contained all the proof, needed of Derek and Tristan's deceit.

I gazed up to the top of the well and spotted the bucket. Did I have time to climb to the top, lower it, and then head back down, to put the book inside, before I was discovered?

"Who's in there?" Derek called from the other end of the tunnel, answering my question.

I prayed to God like never before, at that moment, as I rolled onto my back, pushed the book down into the waist band of my jeans, and then hurriedly pulled my belt, so tight that it dug painfully into my back.

Reaching out with my hands, I felt around the inner wall of the well for one of the footholds and found the wall was now running with water from a downpour that must have begun, while I'd been exploring the hidden rooms.

Finding the foothold I was looking for, I pulled myself out of the hole; scrambling up the side of the now slippery well, as rain pummelled the top of my head. As my hands grew wetter, the climb became harder, as I struggled for grip.

When, at last, I reached the rim of the well, I breathed a sigh of relief; but, as I pulled my head up over the edge, fear gripped me, once more, as I spotted Derek, rushing towards the garden gate.

Tears streaking my face now, I used every ounce of strength I had to pull myself up, over the edge of the well; falling down onto the grass beside it, with a thud.

Spinning around fast, as the old man rushed towards me with surprising speed, I braced myself for his attack; pulling my legs back into my chest for protection. But, as he towered over me, instinct took over; both my legs, shooting out and catching him hard in the groin. As he doubled over with pain, I rolled to the side and sprang to my feet. Bolting towards the low wall, which I was able to jump with ease, I sprinted out across the moors; desperate to get to Jem.

CHAPTER 34

The dark silhouettes of both Rough Tor and Brown Willy were my distant guides, as I stumbled my way across the uneven ground of Bodmin moor, towards the tor that seemed, so far away.

I had been running for almost fifteen minutes, when I heard the sound of an engine, behind me, and was forced to hurriedly change direction. I sprinted towards the fields that lay off to one side of the moors, as fast as I could, knowing that, behind the large, granite walls; I would find protection from my pursuer.

Clambering up the side of one of the these walls, I glanced back and spotted Jem's mother's Land Rover hurriedly approaching, but it was not Jenny at the wheel this time.

I jumped down into the field, praying he had not seen me, but knowing in my heart that he had; the screech of tires, a few seconds later, being all the confirmation I needed to break into a run, once more. I heard a door slam shut a few moments later, but I did not stop.

"I'm not going to hurt you Lizzy. I just want to talk to you; to explain," Derek called into the night, but I refused to stop; reaching the far side of the field and clambering over another wall.

I did not stop until I reached the edge of the second

field. Gasping for breath, I hurriedly tried to think about my options. I knew that I needed to get back onto the moors, in order to get to Rough Tor, but I could still hear Derek Trerise, calling out to me; his voice getting steadily louder.

It was clear that I would have to cut across several fields; some of them surrounded by hedges and not stone walls, in order to get back onto the moor, which would mean travelling a greater distance than I, otherwise, would have, but there was no way I could go back, past Jem's grandfather.

Breaking into a sprint, once more, I flew across the fields, stumbling and tripping in my haste until; my foot, catching on a stone, I flew through the air, smashing down hard on my side. Agonising pain shot up through my left leg and a yelp escaped my lips, before I could stop it.

I gripped my hands to my mouth and listened; trying to gage if he had heard, then hurriedly tried to pull myself up. Biting my lip, as pain coursed through my ankle, I slowly made my way over to a nearby hedge, hurriedly searching for a loose stick that I could use to help support myself; but, there was nothing.

"Where are you, Lizzy?" I heard him call, "You're just like your mother, aren't you? You can't just let things go. You have to keep looking and looking, until you find the answer. Well, your mother had to learn the hard way, and it looks like you will, too," he called.

I wondered what he meant, as I slowly tried to reach the gate; my arms getting slashed to pieces by the brambles, as I clung to the hedge for support.

"They say Reno was dumb," he called, "but he was smart enough to keep his mouth shut; as was your mother, in the end. Are you smart, Lizzy?"

As I reached the gate, I almost cried out with relief, tugging it open; though my relief, soon faded, as it creaked and groaned.

"Oh, I hear you," I heard him call, quickly followed by the thud of heavy footsteps. I knew I had to run; that I could beat him, if I could just stand the pain. It's just a sprain, I told myself, as I forced myself into a jog, tears, springing to my eyes.

"Everyone wants to steal my house, but they didn't have to die. If they'd just agreed to sell..," he called after me then, changing his mind, said, "You don't have to die either, Lizzy; not if you marry my grandson. You could stop all this, now. I promise, I'm not going to hurt you."

At last, I saw the gate that opened onto the moors, and gritting my teeth, I broke into a sprint. Charging through the thankfully open, gate, and out onto the moors, I headed for the looming shadow that was Rough Tor.

Every step was agony, but I forced myself on; the grandfather's words, still carrying to me on the wind, seeming to fade into the distance, as I raced forward. Then, hearing footsteps, ahead of me, I froze; gazing into the pitch black, trying to make out who was there. The footsteps stopped, as soon as I did, and fear rushed over my body. Was it Jem or perhaps someone else, out roaming the moors, in hopes of seeing the elusive, Charlotte?

I was frozen to the spot; afraid to go on, unable to go back, my mind racing, as I tried to think. Then, I heard the grandfather's voice, off in the distance still, but close enough that I, once more, broke into a run, scanning the moors ahead of me; fear, gripping my insides.

It was not long, before I could pick out a figure in the darkness, ahead; just a black shape, at first, but then clearer, and I knew in a flash that, although it was clearly a man, it was not Jem.

As the man lunged towards me, I sprang off to the right; heading down towards the stream, the footsteps of my pursuer, thudding in my ears. I cried out with fear, as the steps got closer and closer, and I knew that I could not outrun him.

He slammed me hard from behind, knocking me to the ground and winding me. I screamed out, as loud as I could, praying my screams would reach Jem or anyone else, who had wandered to the memorial, in hope of seeing Charlotte's ghost; but, I knew that I must, still be at least a mile from Rough Tor, if not more.

I was roughly flipped over. Tristan towered over me, his eyes full of anger, as he dropped down on top of me, pinning my arms, up over my head.

"You should have left well enough alone, Tizzy," he hissed, "You'd have been ok, if you'd have stayed out of it. Gramps wasn't gonna touch you; not as long as you was with Jem or me," he said, and I thought I saw a hint of sadness behind his eyes.

"How much did you read?" he asked, forcing my hands together, so he could free one of his hands and extract the book from my waist band. I fought then, squirming beneath him in the mud, desperate to get free; but, it was no good. He was far stronger than I was and, with ease, he undid my belt, with one hand, and extracted the book.

"It was silly to write it all down, I know, but it feels good to boast of our brilliance; even if it is only in a book. We wanted it to be found, once we were both, long in the grave; to be found and marvelled at. You have to admit my granddad was very clever, Tizzy; all those murders, and yet, still walking free," he said, waving the book at me; a twisted smile, spreading across his face.

"He killed his own brother, Tristan; used and banished his daughter, murdered people that thought he was their friend, and then, let a sick man be punished for his crimes. You think that is something to be proud of? It's sick; he's sick, you're sick!" I yelled, fighting once more, to get free.

Tristan jumped up this time, grabbing for my hair and yanking me up, off the ground, while I screamed out in agony; my hands, flying instantly to my head, desperate to stop the pain. Rain fell, unrelenting; the ground, beneath us, fast becoming a muddy pool, while I scrambled to pull my feet in and push myself up, my efforts, causing me to slide further from his gripping hand, as I felt another wave of pain wash over me.

"Stay still Tizzy, you're only making it worse," he hissed, and then lowered his hands; so, at last, I could sit in the mud, without so much pain.

*

Tristan still had me hard, by the hair, when his grandfather puffed into sight, a few minutes later.

"Where's the book?" Derek snapped instantly, giving me a cursory glance.

"Here," Tristan said, extracting the book from his jacket, where he had stowed it, to protect it from the rain.

The grandfather smiled, crookedly; snatching it from his grandson, before thrusting it inside of his own jacket which he zipped up tight, before turning and glaring at me.

"We'll have to kill her," he said, bluntly, "She won't keep her mouth shut, like her mother did."

"How are we meant to do that, Gramps? I was out looking for ghosts. I didn't expect to be making any," he snapped sarcastically, as he gazed at his grandfather.

"A rock, a stick, I don't care; just cave her head in," the grandfather snapped, snatching for my arm, and shoving Tristan to the ground, laughing raucously, as his grandson fell; face first, into the mud.

"Quickly!" He snapped, once his laughing fit was over, and I watched as Tristan scrambled to his feet; cursing under his breath, as he wiped the mud from his face with his coat sleeve, then began to pace around, searching for a weapon.

I watched nervously, wanting him to get a safe distance away, before I tried to escape his grandfather's grip. I counted his steps, praying and praying for him to find nothing nearby that he could use to harm me; my breath, catching in my throat, as he suddenly stopped and gazed out across the moors. It was then, I heard something, heading towards us, moving fast, panting heavily, and out of nowhere, Beans flew at the grandfather; snapping his jaws on his wrist.

I felt him let go of me and I rolled forward, onto my hands and knees, slipping and sliding in the mud, as I tried to stand up; the old man's screams, echoing in my ears, mingled with the collie's snarls, as I, at last, found my footing and sprinted off across the moors, once more, whistling for Beans. Then, out of nowhere, Bailey flew at me; panic in his eyes, and I had to jump out of the way, to avoid a collision.

"Come on!" I yelled; not stopping, but sprinting on, Beans, right beside me, matching my pace, while Bailey shot past us both, his tail between his legs.

I could hear Tristan's heavy footsteps; hear him, getting closer and closer, his speed, way outpacing mine.

"I'll set the dogs on you!" I cried, desperate to make him stop, but he kept coming.

I tried to pick up the pace, but my ankle screamed out in protest.

Then, seeing a stick on the ground, I snatched it up and spun around, smashing it into the side of Tristan's head. Gasping, I dropped it instantly, shocked that he had been so close.

Beans barked, frantically, as Tristan grasped at his head.

"You fucking bitch!" He snarled, grabbing for the stick, before I had time to realise my mistake. I spun on my heels, but he smashed the stick into my bad ankle, sending me sprawling to the ground, then yelled at Beans and Bailey, who were both barking at him, viciously.

Beans instantly dropped to the ground and I realised that he had, no doubt, taken orders from Tristan, before and, having known him, longer than me, was bound to listen to him, but Bailey had no intention of doing the same. His back up; he stood between Tristan and me, snarling threateningly, his fear, it seemed, replaced with a desperate need to protect me. However, Bailey was still not fully grown and no match for Tristan, who slammed the stick hard, into his side, sending him flying, while I scrambled to go after him.

"I'm going to enjoy this," Tristan said, stamping down hard on my ankle; the loud crack of the bone breaking, followed instantly by agonising pain.

I screamed out, my head spinning, as slowly my vision began to blur and then, just as I was sure the stick would come crashing down, I heard a yell, saw Tristan's head shoot up, gazing past me, across the moors, and then Jem's voice calling out, "Have him, Beans!"

Beans flew at Tristan, knocking him to the ground. I fought to pull myself through the rain, towards the shape of my beautiful pup, the pain, causing my head to spin and my vision to blur. Then, exhausted and no longer able to fight, I let my eyes close and drifted into oblivion.

CHAPTER 35

I woke in the hospital with my father and Jem sitting beside my bed, watching me nervously; smiles coming to rest on their faces, as they saw me gazing back at them.

"Hi, beautiful," they said in unison, then looked at each other and smiled.

I smiled back, everything a blur; my mind, working hard to remember something, something important, but I couldn't quite remember what. I rubbed at my eyes, gazed at Jem, who was covered in Mud, and suddenly I remembered; the moors, Derek, Tristan, the dogs.

My eyes grew wide, as I remembered my pup; my beautiful pup, so viciously smashed in the side. Tears instantly sprang to my eyes, but I could not bring myself to speak; so afraid was I of what I might be told.

"Tiz," both Jem and my father said, as they moved to stand, both pausing to gaze at each other briefly with uncertainty; my father eventually sitting back down, giving Jem permission to go on.

"Tiz," he said again, coming closer and perching on the side of the bed, where he could gently stroke my hair with one hand, the other reaching forward to gently caress my hand, "It's ok, everything's alright now. You're safe," he continued, looking to my father for reassurance.

"But, Bailey," I sobbed, "he..."

"He's fine," Jem said, hurriedly.

"Just a little sore," my father added, quickly; smiling across at me.

"Did you forget you have the best vet in town for a father?" Jem asked, playfully; but I could detect the sadness in his voice.

"You saved me," I said, smiling up at him and gripping his hand tighter in way of a thank you.

"No," he replied, shaking his head; his expression, sad for a moment, before he forced a smile to his face, "Beans and that pup of yours did most of the work. Hell, if they hadn't run off on me like that, I wouldn't have had a clue what was going on," he said, turning his head away, as if ashamed.

"You should have talked to us," my father interjected, seeing Jem's pain and moving around to the other side of the bed, where he took my free hand, "If you'd have told me what you found in your mother's diary..," he began, but I cut him off mid-sentence.

"You'd have told me you knew about the rooms and to just forget about it," I said, daring him, with my eyes, to deny it.

"Maybe," he said, "but, if you'd said something about the banging and the voices, Tiz, I might have got suspicious and gone looking."

"But, that was before I knew about the rooms. I didn't want you to think you'd made the wrong choice in moving to Insane Reno. I knew how important the surgery was to you. I wasn't going to be like mum."

"I know," he replied, tears forming behind his eyes, "but your mum was right, Tiz; I did put you at risk. I can't bear to think what might have happened, if those dogs hadn't heard you and gone running."

It was then, I remembered Tristan and Derek Trerise and, looking to Jem, who was facing me, once more, I asked, "What happened with your brother and your grandfather?"

"They're locked up," he said, looking sad, "The police have both your mother's and my grandfather's diaries"

"My mums?" I asked, perplexed.

"I knew your mum must have told you about the rooms," my father jumped in, "I was so mad at her that I called, to have it out with her. She told me, she hadn't told you anything and then she said that her dairy had gone missing, recently. It wasn't hard to put two and two together, Tiz."

At my guilty expression, my father turned to Jem and instructed him to go on with what he had been saying.

"The police took both my grandfather and Tristan away. I didn't read much of their twisted tale, but what I did read was enough to tell me the truth about them both, and when the police have read the whole thing, I suspect my grandfather won't be getting anymore tastes of freedom. As for Tristan, I'm not sure. Technically, he didn't kill anyone; but, he intended to. He made that perfectly clear in their dairy. I guess we'll just have to wait and see what happens, when it goes to court."

"Are you okay?" I asked, realising how hard it must be for him to discover the truth about his family; because, although he hated Tristan, he had loved his grandfather, had trusted him, as most kids would a grandparent, and so this had to be a shock for him.

"You're okay and that's all that matters to me," he said, leaning down and kissing my hand, "You had me worried for a while there, though, when you wouldn't wake up; but, they say it was just a mixture of pain and exhaustion that knocked you out and, other than a broken leg and some cuts and bruises, you're gonna be just fine."

I laid there in that hospital bed and smiled up at the two men I loved most, thankful that I, at last, knew the truth; that finally, Insane Reno's horrific past was fully out in the open, and that, after all, justice truly would be done.

I just wished that Reno had still been alive to see it.

EPILOGUE

A year later

Things are almost back to normal now. My father's practice is doing well and I was accepted into a great veterinary school. I miss home, the animals, and Jem, of course, but visit them often. Jem's grandfather and his brother were sent to prison for their crimes; their shared diary of events, used as evidence to convict them.

Although, Derek will live the rest of his life behind bars, Tristan could be out in just five years. After all, he did not actually commit any murders, only broke my ankle; an injury that is no longer causing me problems. We're told this is actually a good sentence; considering. Jem's grandfather, however, received several life sentences, as it was revealed, through his Diary, that he had murdered eight people; most of them, members of the Yelland family. They are as follows: Bert and Patience Yelland, James Trerise, who was Derek's own brother, Martin and Audrey Yelland, Matthew and Julie Yelland, and lastly, Tom Richards.

With the true culprit behind bars, at last, my father decided that it was time our home be given back its original name of Moorview Farm, which we had discovered by reading a collection of journals, written by Edward Trerise, the first owner of the house and the man responsible for it being built. However, I suspect it may never truly shake off its nickname of Insane Reno.

The house itself had its own very interesting history, even before the murders took place; having been built in the eighteen hundreds with one thing in mind, smuggling.

Edward Trerise proved to be a very clever, if somewhat unethical, man; even going so far as to create the perfect room for his deceased child, supposedly as a shrine to her memory, when, in fact, it was simply to cover his illicit dealings, by further helping to minimise the risks of his secret rooms, beneath the house, being discovered. The true purpose of this hidden bedroom door was to provide an easy escape from the main house into the hidden rooms below for his cohorts, should the authorities come calling, when he and his men were making plans.

However, this was not how the smuggler's goods entered the house. You see, the smugglers would come to the house late at night; one man, climbing down to the bottom of the well, where he would stand on a large block that was hidden beneath the water. The items stolen from the wrecked ships would then be lowered down to this man, who would set them, one at a time, onto the small trolley, which I had seen the day I crawled along the tunnel to the hidden rooms. This would then be pulled along the tunnel, using a pulley system; the floor cleverly sloped at the corner to help it easily move around the turn. Once unloaded, the man would then pull the trolley back and repeat the process. At the other end, several men would work; moving the items quickly into the hidden rooms and small storages areas off of the main rooms. It was a cleverly thought out system.

Looking at the house now, the position of the well may very well seem strange, placed at the front of the house as it is, but originally this would have been the back of the house; the door at the side, leading out onto the yard, having been the original front door.

The carts, loaded with their stolen goods, would come in along tracks to the back of the house, avoiding the more commonly used route towards the front, and were hidden from view, should anyone come across from the Rough Tor direction, while they worked.

Even the living room had been a pre-planned design; the L-shape, allowing for both the front and back of the house to be viewed, so that trouble could be quickly spotted and a warning given to the men at the rear of the house, within seconds.

Also, the wall that now surrounded the small garden area is never mentioned, which suggests this was added at a later date.

The smuggling in Cornwall, at the time, would have been terrible; ships being guided towards the rocks on purpose and the crews killed, so that the ships could be looted. Places such as Insane Reno and the famous, Jamaica Inn, provided the perfect hiding place for the cargo that was stolen.

It soon became apparent that Jem's ancestor had not been happy to stop at stolen goods, as he became heavily addicted to drinking and gambling; frequently taking great risks with his property and the people around him, even going so far as to offer up his wife and his home in wagers. His journals depicted an array of bizarre wagers, such as whether or not it would rain within the following week, who would be victorious in a fight, and even bets based around how quickly he could reduce his wife to tears.

The wife of this cruel man, however, is rarely mentioned; except, it seems, for when he wished to relay a cruel trick or punishment that he had placed on her, or a wager, in which he had set her as the prize. It seems, from what he does write, that she was considerably younger than him and quite beautiful, making her an ideal prize, when his funds were low and he was craving a gambling fix.

Of course, he went on to lose everything; his wife and his home, because of his addiction. His anger and rage at this is clear in his journals; an anger and rage, which it seems, passed on to a young Derek Trerise, when he discovered the hidden rooms, over a decade later.

Ironically, it seems that Derek is going to get his wish, after all, as Jem and I are now engaged and with our marriage, the house is guaranteed to pass into the hands of a Trerise, once again. However, I am confident that this Trerise will be a little less corrupt.

But, the story doesn't end there, as my father, now divorced from my mother, has fallen in love, once again; this time with a woman who shares many of his own hopes and dreams and who is, like himself, a vet.

He and Alison are very much in love and Dad tells me that he hopes to propose to her in the, not too distant, future. I couldn't be happier. So, it seems that there will be two marriages in the Bray's future.

Mother, however, did not do so well in her relationship with Imelda's father. On discovering that she had been aware of Reno's innocence and still allowed him to be accused, Mr Thomas decided that mum was not as perfect, as he had once thought and that she was, in fact, a bad influence for his beloved daughter, and so he terminated the relationship. Mum now lives in a small house in Bude, paid for by my father. Well, he's too kind for his own good, sometimes.

Then there is Emily; forced to stay away from her family for years, she is now, once again, reunited with her brother and his family.

As for Morwena; well, she is still getting spoiled, only now, it's her long lost aunt, who is the spoiler, paying for her to go to singing lessons and pursue her dream of being a singer. She's also happily dating Martin, who is one love sick puppy.

There is still, so much more I wish to learn about

Insane Reno and the murders that took place here; but for now, I'm going to focus on my studies and achieving my dreams. Everything else, I hope, is history.

THANK YOU!

To my Reader: Many thanks for purchasing and reading my book, I hope you enjoyed it.

If you did enjoy reading it, please post a review at Amazon and let your friends know about *Insane Reno.*

Happy Reading!
All the best

Jossie

ACKNOWLEDGEMENTS

How do I even begin to thank the people who have made this, my first novel, possible? There are so many who have touched my heart, throughout my life, and encouraged me to follow my dream of becoming a published author; from family to friends, teachers, and even brief acquaintances.

With so many to thank, I apologise to all those, who are not mentioned here, but know that I love you all and that I am so thankful for all the amazing friends and family members in my life; especially those no longer with me, I miss you guys. You have all helped to make sure I was never truly alone and I am so blessed to know so many amazing people.

So, to begin with, I have to thank my husband, Dan, who has worked hard every day for almost nine years to support our little family, and in doing so, has enabled me to remain home to write and care for our wonderful son, Kye. I can honestly not thank you enough for your support, love, and hours of entertainment that helped to keep me smiling at even the most difficult times. You are a wonderful man, husband and father. We are both so proud of you and I know your grandparents would be proud of you, too. You're our rock; ever dependable, and Kye and I will always love you. You were always so sure I'd get here in the end and you sacrificed so much in order to help me achieve this, so again, thank you; not only for that, but for coping with my brilliant ability to destroy laptops and my insistence that I must have another one, right now, my moments of complete meltdown, and my frequent episodes of blondness.

Special mention goes out to Samantha Bell, my tireless cheerleader, who has read through many of my articles, manuscripts, and short stories, over the years, and has always had an unwavering faith in my ability to one day become a published author; even when my faith in myself was lacking. Thanks for the laughter, love, and even the times when you've been viciously blunt in telling it to me straight. Who'd have thought two scruffy, animal mad three year olds, just getting to know each other, could and would grow up to achieve so many of their dreams? Love you Wammy.

To Ninny, mother of Wammy, thank you for getting your pest of a daughter out of bed in the early hours of the morning to go and walk dogs with me. If I'd have known, all those years ago that it was you, hearing my pebble throwing and not Wammy, I'd have just knocked on the front door instead. Also, a big thank you for all the times you've driven her to mine. The way you are as a mother and with your friends has been an inspiration to me and I promise to do my best to be there for Sam, long after you are gone, which I am hoping will not be for an extremely long time, because I'm pretty certain she's going to be hard work without you around to keep her in line.

To my mum; life hasn't always been easy, but you've taught me never to give up, no matter the challenges we face. Thank you for all the dreams you left behind in order to help all of us achieve ours. I know I don't say it enough, but I do love you.

My beautiful son, Kye, light of my life, my biggest achievement; you are and always will be an inspiration to me, always smiling, laughing and loving. You're my little angel, sent from God and I adore you.

To my past teachers, Mrs Frost, Mrs Gilbert, Mrs Chapman, and all the rest; thank you from the bottom of my heart. You believed in me, challenged me and never gave up on me; even when I had all but given up on myself. Insane Reno would not be finished today, if it were not for you. You showed me I could achieve anything I set my mind to and I am truly and eternally grateful.

To dad, thank you for the only peas I ever liked, fresh from the pods, for collecting pebbles with me on the beach, and the feral kitten you spent hours trying to catch, and lastly Cornwall, surely the greatest gift any father could give his family; a childhood of freedom and exploration. Without you, I'd never have been able to find and fall in love with Bodmin Moor and this book never could have been. Love you.

To Lisa Solheim, I am so lucky to have such an amazing sister-in-law, who is so supportive of me and my work. You will never know how much I adore you; unless, of course, you get me excessively drunk, again.

To Jean Sisson, my wonderful mother-in-law, who has boosted my ego immensely, since I got my publishing deal and who has the potential to make me the happiest woman alive, by destroying a certain embarrassing video. Thank you so much for being there and supporting me in both the birth of this book and the birth of that little monster we both love, so much, Kye Kye, and also for bringing my wonderful husband and sister-in-law into the world. Love you.

Thanks also go out to all the puppy dogs in my life, big and small, who have touched my heart in so many ways, and other animals, too.

Then there is Dave Lyons at Raven Crest Books. I do not know you all that well, as of yet, but hope to get to. Thank you for giving me this amazing opportunity. May Insane Reno be the first of many books we publish together. A thank you also to anyone, who has a part in taking this book from my computer screen out into the world.

And last, but far from least, Chuck Jolly. How do I even begin to thank you? You lifted me up when I was low, gave tirelessly of your time, pushed and encouraged me, whenever I doubted myself, and have had faith in me, the likes of which, I have never known. You have been a best friend, father figure, Grampie, editor, and champion; all, thrown into one, and never let me give up. You know Insane Reno as well as I do, and together this book has been our baby. Well, we did it Grampie. You were right all along; as if there was ever any doubt. You are and always will be an amazing man and I hope I will always be the craziest little English girl in your life. Good thing, I'm cute, right? Love you Grampie.

CONTACT DETAILS

Blog: joss-dreamingofpublication.blogspot.co.uk

Facebook: www.facebook.com/jossie.marie

Twitter: twitter.com/Jossiemarie84

Second Life: jossie Tyrellium

Cover design by: Jossie Marie Solheim

Published by: Raven Crest Books:
www.ravencrestbooks.com

Follow us on Twitter:
www.twitter.com/lyons_dave

Facebook:
www.facebook.com/ravencrestbooksclub

CPSIA information can be obtained at www.ICGtesting.com
Printed in the USA
LVOW01s1704300714

396753LV00021B/861/P

9 781480 071209